AND THEN THE RAIN STOPPED

AND THEN THE RAIN STOPPED

Nan Maynard

Chivers Press
Bath, England

G.K. Hall & Co.
Thorndike, Maine USA

This Large Print edition is published by Chivers Press, England, and by G.K. Hall & Co., USA.

Published in 1998 in the U.K. by arrangement with Robert Hale Ltd.

Published in 1998 in the U.S. by arrangement with Robert Hale Ltd.

U.K. Hardcover ISBN 0–7540–3276–0 (Chivers Large Print)
U.K. Softcover ISBN 0–7540–3277–9 (Camden Large Print)
U.S. Softcover ISBN 0–7838–0117–3 (Nightingale Series Edition)

The text of this Large Print edition is unabridged.
Other aspects of the book may vary from the original edition.

Set in 16 pt. New Times Roman.

Printed in Great Britain on acid-free paper.

British Library Cataloguing in Publication Data available

Library of Congress Cataloging-in-Publication Data

Maynard, Nan.
And then the rain stopped / by Nan Maynard.
p. cm.
ISBN 0-7838-0117-3 (lg. print : sc : alk. paper)
1. Large type books. I. Title.
[PR6063.A889A8 1998]
823'.914—dc21 98-2819

This book is dedicated, with best wishes, to Fred Atkins who grew suddenly younger on the 26th May 1983

CHAPTER ONE

Hilary French stood outside the chapel looking over at the small group of mourners bending over the flowers, like black crows, she thought, nodding and murmuring to each other as they read the cards.

Inside the chapel she had been uncomfortably aware of the curious, even hostile, looks of the women, the grudging admiration in the eyes of the men and told herself she should have dressed down for this occasion, the funeral of her ex-husband. Instead, here she was in her chic black and white pillbox, model suit and custom-made shoes showing the world the well known glossy image of Hilary French, owner of exclusive fashion salons in London, Manchester and Paris. She was so conspicuous in this gathering that even the vicar and pall-bearers sent her glances of open enquiry.

As she stood there she looked away from the mourners and stared in macabre fascination at the curl of smoke rising from the crematorium. Surely, she thought, in these enlightened days they could have a less distressing system. She wondered why she had come to the funeral of a man she had ceased to love or need years ago. Was it guilt that brought her here, at least to pay one last act of homage to Graham French who had given her his name and her three daughters? That's all he gave me, she thought, the rest I did for myself.

'Well, Hilary?' said a quiet voice behind her.

Hilary turned and looked into the tired face of the widow. Myrtle French, she knew, was her own age—forty-three—but whereas Hilary knew *she* didn't look a day over thirty, Myrtle French looked much older than her years. Her ugly black hat showed up her sallow complexion and her tight black coat accentuated the thickening of her figure—a nondescript woman—her only claim to distinction the stark misery on her face.

'Hello Myrtle,' said Hilary 'it was good of you to let me know the arrangements. It must have been a dreadful shock for you.'

'Sudden death is always shocking,' said the widow.

'Yes.' Hilary looked away from the grief and accusation in Myrtle French's eyes. She didn't know what to say next.

'How are your girls?'

Hilary looked back at her, grateful for the opening.

'Very well, thank you. As you probably know, Lana's been married five years now and has twin daughters of three. Maxine runs my home and does accounting work for the salons and Cleo works with me in the London salon.'

A bleak smile twisted the widow's lips. 'I read about you and your three daughters in a fashion magazine recently, a stable of elegant thoroughbreds they called you.'

Hilary gave an apologetic smile. 'They tend to be stupidly extravagant in their phrasing sometimes.'

The other mourners were looking now with open curiosity at the two women—the two wives of the deceased.

'Well, Hilary,' said Myrtle, 'have you found fame and fortune adequate compensation for driving away a man who loved you?'

Hilary wished more than ever that she'd stayed away from Graham's funeral. She had no desire to enter into this sort of conversation with his widow.

'He left me for *you*,' she pointed out quietly.

'To keep his self respect.' There was open bitterness in the widow's voice now. 'He never stopped loving you, Hilary. You were in our bed every single night of our marriage.' She opened her plastic handbag and took out a snapshot which she pressed into Hilary's gloved hand. 'You'd better have this. I found it in his wallet after his death.'

Before Hilary could reply, Myrtle French walked over to the cars, the other mourners straggling after her. Hilary looked down at the picture in her hand. Herself and Graham French at his insurance company's annual dinner just after their marriage. The picture was faded and torn at the edges but the love light in the eyes of the boy and girl was still plain to see. Her thoughts spun back to the past, but the past was dead. She could find nothing in her heart for Graham French. It had died years ago.

Still holding the picture she watched the cars drive away and was startled when a silver Citröen CX Turbo skidded to a halt behind her.

Her son-in-law, Rory Jefferson, got out and strolled towards her in leisurely fashion—a strange contrast to the speed and dash of his driving. As always, Hilary was irritated by the man-woman chemistry that swung into action in Rory's presence. She was angry, too, that he was only too well aware of it. Rory Jefferson needed no one to tell him that he was attractive to women of all ages. Again as always, Hilary's clothes sense appreciated his appearance. It was a mild December day and Rory's well-tailored sports jacket was open revealing a sleek polo-necked cashmere sweater. Grafter and wide boy he might be, but he had all the confidence and presence of an aristocrat. Rory Jefferson, he described himself, the only Scottish Cockney in the business. Yes, thought Hilary now, I can see why Lana married him instead of one of the conservative young men she was brought up with.

'Hi, mother-in-law, you look like you've lost a bob and found a tanner, as me old Grandad used to say. Hey, someone upset you?' he asked, quizzing at the picture in her hand. Hastily Hilary dropped it into her black patent-leather handbag.

'Someone just told me the truth,' she said, 'and it wasn't pleasant. Anyway, what brings *you* here?'

'Just thought I'd see if Lana changed her mind about attending her dad's funeral.'

'You should know Lana better than that,' said Hilary, 'after all, you're an expert on women, aren't you?'

He grinned. 'Yeh. Specially those with pepper on their tongues. Black suits you, Hilary.'

'Thanks.'

'Where's your car?'

'I came by taxi. I should have kept it. Now I have to ring for another.'

'Have lunch with me.'

'No, thanks. I'm going back to the salon.'

'But it's Monday. The salon doesn't open on Mondays and you've got to have lunch somewhere.' He took her arm and turned her to face him. 'Look, Hilary, would it hurt you so much? You know I don't hold my meat knife like a fish knife and I don't push my plate away when I've finished and I don't tuck my napkin into my collar.'

She smiled faintly. 'What a snob you are.'

'So you don't have to approve of me to have lunch with me. Anyway, I'm glad you don't approve of me. It makes it more exciting.'

'For whom?'

'For both of us.' He let go of her arm. 'If you

won't lunch with me I shan't drive you to a 'phone box to ring for a taxi and your shoes weren't built to tramp on that gravel. I bet you'd feel the stones through the soles.'

Hilary was tempted. 'I should have brought my car.'

'But you didn't, Hilary, and you look like you could use a drink.'

'Several.'

'That's my girl.'

After the first martini Rory drank plain tonic. On *her* third martini Hilary said, 'Do you intend your marriage to Lana to last?'

He was startled by the abrupt question but he answered calmly. 'For ever.'

'But you've divorced one wife.'

'I'd have divorced Susie even if I hadn't met Lana. I outgrew her.' He stared at her levelly. 'Like you outgrew *yours*.'

Hilary sighed.

'I didn't mean to rob the girls of a father, but my success destroyed Graham. It made him feel a failure, although I never treated him as one. He wanted to come into the business with me, but I knew he'd mess it up. He would have been too timid to take chances, too soft with staff. Graham could never make waves, he was a cautious man with no ambitions.' As if talking to herself Hilary went on in a cold, flat voice. 'After Lana was born I went back to work in the sweat shop and my mother looked after Lana. I had to work. Graham's money was not enough.

Then one day I had to take a message into the office of my boss. He told me to enter, then ignored me as his wife was with him ranting and raving at him. She was young, a quarter his age and very lovely. You could see she'd never wear any of the rubbish we turned out in her husband's sweat shop. I stood there while she shouted at him reviling all the famous dress designers you could name. 'None of the idiots,' she screamed at him, 'have the remotest idea of what I want. For an occasion like this I must have something sensational. I don't give a damn whether it's in fashion or not.' Anyway, eventually I gave him the message and when I got home that night I designed a dress that I knew would suit his wife's nineteen-twenty-ish beauty. I even stated the colours and material in which it should be made. Next day, heart in mouth, I took it in to him. After that I never looked back. I engaged a nursemaid for Lana and by the time Maxine and Cleo were born the household ran on oiled wheels. I went up in the fashion world and Graham still peddled his insurance. He grew more and more sullen. I couldn't make him see I was content with the situation so the rows got worse and worse. There were nasty scenes, bad for the girls to hear. I thought it would sort itself out, but it didn't. I get the feeling that all three girls would have been happier if we'd still been living in a three-up, three-down in Balham.'

'Don't you believe it,' said Rory, 'the stupid

bitches might pretend they would, but they'd hate it, particularly Lana with her million dollar ideas. They ought to be bloody grateful.'

Hilary gave the ghost of a smile. 'I don't want their gratitude. I've learnt to live without it.' She gave a deep sigh. 'When Graham left me we tried sharing the girls. His new wife wouldn't have them in her house so he used to visit us and take them out. Then, as the girls grew older, they had other things to do and used to resent having to give them up to go to the zoo or out to tea with a man they called "Father" but who had become almost a stranger to them. Eventually he stopped coming. They didn't seem to miss him. They had everything they wanted. I tried. I never sent them away to school.' She put down her glass and stood up suddenly. 'Somehow it went wrong. Anyway, enough of boozer's gloom. Shall we eat?'

During the meal they talked of Rory's new property deals and his sale of a site to a large supermarket concern but when they were on their coffee he switched abruptly from business to personalities.

'Maxine's not like you or Lana or Cleo. Does she take after her father?'

'Yes,' said Hilary, 'Maxine's like Graham, gentle, caring, but absolutely no ambition. People like Graham and Maxine are born to be martyrs. I hope she won't get hurt the way Graham did.'

'Lana's like you,' said Rory, 'bags of class and slave to no man.'

'Is that why you married her,' asked Hilary, 'because of her class?'

His eyes glinted with amusement. 'Do I hear the sophisticated Hilary French clucking mother hen noises all of a sudden over her baby chicks?'

'Oh, don't be so bloody cute,' snapped Hilary.

Rory grinned. 'How about another brandy, mother-in-law?'

'Don't keep calling me that. You make me feel ninety.'

'You don't look ninety.' His voice dropped caressingly. 'Twenty, more like.'

'And don't flirt with me either. I'm not a dewy-eyed teenager.'

'I don't go for dewy-eyed teenagers.'

Her eyes grew troubled as she sipped her second brandy. 'I'm worried about Cleo's obsession with those degenerate twins, Bunny and Polly Jameson. At nineteen a girl is so vulnerable.'

'Don't lose any sleep over Cleo,' said Rory, his eyes hardening. 'Cleo's a match for the Jamesons.'

He smiled a grim, secret smile. Ever since his marriage to Lana when Cleo was only fourteen, he'd known how she felt about him. Cleo was hot for men just like his randy, slutty mother had been and Rory Jefferson would never be brought down by women like his mother. He hated them with an intensity foreign to his normally casual attitude to life. Meantime, it amused him to play Cleo's game, to watch her delude herself that he treated her with teasing antagonism because she disturbed him sexually. How she postured and challenged him, the hot little bitch, and how he enjoyed playing up to her and letting her bask in her supposed power over him and, one day, when the time was ripe, he would finally destroy her fantasy and humiliate her as his father should have humiliated his mother. When the moment of truth was brought home to Cleo, it would be like kicking his mother in the teeth. An exultant feeling ran through him almost like the urge of sex. He came out of his melée of bitter thoughts to find Hilary dreamily appraising the discreet Christmas decorations that adorned the luxurious restaurant.

'I applaud the good taste,' she murmured, 'nothing cheap or gaudy about *these* decorations.'

Rory grinned. 'Christmas has come a long way since that grotty old stable.'

'And you,' she said abruptly, her smile fading, 'you've come a long way, too, haven't you?'

For Rory this was a day of surprises. Never before had his mother-in-law talked to him this way. After the first shock of Lana's decision to marry him, Hilary had treated him with a faintly contemptuous tolerance, but never had she made him feel like one of the family.

'Yes, I've come a bloody long way,' he said, 'and the only way from here is up. We're two of a kind, Hilary, although you may not be exactly mad about the idea.' His eyes held hers and the magnetism of him, as always, troubled her senses. 'I clawed my way up,' he said, 'and no man's ever gonna put me down.'

'And no woman either?' she asked lightly, thinking with faint unease of the way he sometimes was with Cleo.

'No woman either. I have all I want with Lana and the kids, but what about *you*, Hilary? Do you intend to go on alone? Time will come when Maxine and Cleo will go, then there'll be just you and Clarrie. Clarrie may be an excellent housekeeper but . . .' his eyebrows quirked up, 'isn't it time now for you to stop and think where you go from here apart from the businesses?'

A slight smile curved her mouth. 'Like a man, I suppose? I drove one away once, remember?'

'He was a fool,' said Rory softly. 'A real man would have stayed and put you in the passenger seat.'

'But I like to drive.'

He put a hand briefly over hers. 'Drivers get tired,' he said, 'eventually.'

CHAPTER TWO

Polly Jameson drifted into the bedroom and picked up a fun-fur jacket from the back of a chair. Draping it round her shoulders she stood looking down at her brother—Bunny—lying naked on the bed. Cleo French, also naked, stretched sideways across his legs.

'God!' Polly said, 'this room reeks of pot and sex.'

Cleo reared up and stared at her with stormy eyes.

'Don't go out. Come to bed, Poll.'

'Sorry,' said Polly, 'no can do. I sold a picture yesterday so I'm gonna get me some new gear. *Not* from Hilary French, Hilary French fashions bore me.'

'Me too,' said Cleo, 'I wish you'd come to bed, Polly, just for half an hour, please.'

'Sorry. After I've shopped I'm lunching with my new black mate, Chloe Rodgerson, now is she one horny babe who really turns me on.'

Polly bent down and slapped her twin's ankles.

'Hadn't you better hit the road, lover? Daddy'll get his balls in a twist if you don't see those punters in Cambridge today.'

Bunny pushed Cleo off him and sat up.

'I hate the bloody job, hate it. I'm nothing more than a lousy rep.'

Polly smiled at him. 'Agreed, my pet, you *are*

one hell of a lousy rep. Pity Daddy isn't trading in ladies' porn underwear. That would be much more in your line than electrical goods. You can't get turned on by a hi-fi, or can you? Well, don't say I didn't warn you, Cleo.'

When Polly had gone Cleo nuzzled her face into the pillow which still held Polly's perfume. It gave Cleo sexual fantasies to inhale Polly's scent and think about Polly and Bunny sharing the flat and this bed.

She rolled over and picked up Bunny's watch from the bedside table.

'He's probably all burnt up by now, just a pile of ashes.' She giggled. 'I wonder if mother and his wife will quarrel about who has the ashes.'

Bunny took the watch from her and slipped it over his hand.

'What *are* you talking about?'

'It was my father's funeral this morning.'

Bunny yawned. 'You don't say.'

'He walked out on us and mother. Got sick of taking hand-outs from her.' Cleo gave a great sigh. 'Like me. I want things of my own . . .'

Wearily Bunny interrupted her. 'You don't do so badly. New car every year, clothes, jewellery . . .'

'All hand-outs from mother and if I say anything she brings me down by telling me I'm just another shop-girl. She's mad because I didn't go on a modelling course.'

Bunny ran his hand down her thigh. 'Why didn't you? You've got the looks and the figure.'

'And be taught to walk by some raddled old has-been, compete with a load of skinny, patronising bitches, do you mind?'

Bunny shrugged. 'So stay a shop-girl.' He gave a curt laugh, 'Some shop-girl, swanning round that ritzy salon wearing model clothes and expensive perfumes, youngest daughter of the elegant Hilary French, how did that magazine describe you? Cleo French, that delectable fizz of fashion. It's not exactly shawl, clogs and cold stone mill floor for *you*, is it?'

Bunny lit a joint, took a pull, then handed it to her. She took a toke and handed it back to him. 'She'd kill me if she knew I smoked pot.'

'Can't think why you don't get a place of your own.'

'She doesn't pay me enough to get the kind of apartment I'd like with maid service. I need money. Lots of it.'

'Who doesn't?' Bunny put a hand between her legs and stroked. 'What about that old Hollywood fart you've been screwing? Didn't he come across?'

'Bart Raglan?' Cleo gave a snort of disgust. 'You gotta be joking. He thought being seen around with him was sufficient payment. The dishiest male ever stepped out of Hollywood, the paper said.' She giggled. 'The only way he could get it up was by making me pretend to be his English nanny and smack his bottom and order him to eat his carrots. Maybe I could sell that to the papers.'

'He's gone back to the States,' Bunny said, 'to marry for the fourth time. It was in this morning's paper.'

'I know. Bunny . . .'

'What?'

'What age were you when you had your first sex?'

'Fourteen, with my mother's best friend. Then I taught Poll.'

'I was fifteen,' Cleo said. 'It was after Coral Blake's party.'

Sometimes Cleo shed tears when she was remembering, sometimes she felt hatred for her mother, like now. Never would she forget the joy she'd felt over Coral Blake's party because that day mother would have to take her to the party and collect her afterwards. There was no one else. Clarrie had a sprained wrist and couldn't drive, Maxine was in hospital having her wisdom teeth out and Lana was married and living at Marshwick in the Thames Valley. So, for the first time, it would have to be mother. Cleo would arrive at the party with a mother who was loads prettier and smarter than any of the other mothers. How proud Cleo would be. She hugged herself in anticipation as she got out of bed that morning. Then at breakfast there was mother standing by the table dressed in her mink jacket, a small suitcase on the floor beside her.

'Ah, there you are, darling. I had a call last night after you'd gone to bed. I have to fly over to Paris this morning but Clarrie will get a taxi for you to take you to the party and Coral's mother has promised that someone will bring you home.' Well, someone did bring her home.

'Coral Blake's grandfather was my first,' she said to Bunny. 'He took me into the woods on the way home from the party.'

'Is this confession time or something?'

She tweaked the hairs on his chest. 'Yes, because you're my familiar, like the witch's cat or rather the witch's rat.'

Bunny put the unfinished joint in an ashtray beside the bed and closed his eyes. Cleo snuggled down beside him. It was think time now, the time to stay quiet and think of Rory. She had never talked to Bunny or Polly about Rory. One day they would have to know but Cleo would need to have other men before she got Rory, just to let him know how desirable she was to other men. Rory would keep for, say another five years or so when his marriage to Lana had become really stale. In the meantime there was the love-hate game that only she and Rory knew about. It was exciting and stimulating, better than any of the hash Bunny dreamed up. She closed her eyes to dream and wondered if Rory ever dreamed this way too.

CHAPTER THREE

Lana Jefferson smiled as she heard the sound of her daughters' laughter in the kitchen of her mother's North London home.

'Good old Clarrie, she always takes the twins off me the minute we get here. She knows I'm not madly maternal.'

Of the three sisters, twenty-four year old Lana was the one most like her mother. Both Hilary and Lana had the patrician beauty that made heads turn as they passed, looks that suggested rich furs, gleaming jewels, expensive cocktail bars. Maxine French, at twenty-two, had similar looks, but was slightly darker and her features not so definite, making her a shadowy replica of the other two. She moved less confidently than her mother and elder sister, and her voice was quieter.

'What did mother wear for the funeral?'

'The black suit from Paris,' replied Maxine, 'and that black and white pillbox hat.'

'She just had to go, didn't she, to show that poor old bag, Myrtle, what the best-dressed woman is wearing.'

'I don't think it was that,' said Maxine. 'I think she felt she ought to go. I suppose we should have gone, too.'

'Why?' said Lana, 'he was nothing to us, didn't even remember our birthdays.' She pointed suddenly to some knitting on the settee.

'What you making now? Chest warmers for the vicar?'

'No. A sweater for poor little Patsy Maxwell.'

'Poor mite. Does she miss her mother?'

'Not so much as we feared. You see, Gail was in hospital for long spells before they sent her home to die.' Maxine gave a wan smile. 'I little thought when the vicar asked me in the Parade Post Office to help with the jumble sale that Gail Maxwell and I would become such close friends. Gail was so happy then. Patsy was three months old and Gail was just getting into the swing of things around here, you know, WI and all that.'

Lana gave a mock shudder. 'Sounds ghastly.'

Maxine smiled faintly. 'It was Gail's scene. She was a lovely, caring person before the cancer struck her down.'

'It must have been deadly for you,' said Lana, 'having to go round to that house every day to watch her die.'

'She needed me,' said Maxine simply, 'we used to make plans for when she got better, although I think she knew she was going to die. Also my sitting with her took some of the pressure off Alan's aunt Molly who moved in to take over when Gail was first taken ill.'

'And he's an airline pilot based at Heathrow.'

'Yes.' A faint colour suffused Maxine's face. Lana looked at her sharply.

'How old is he?'

Her voice low, Maxine replied, 'Thirty, I think.'

'So he's very eligible.'

Maxine's head shot up, the colour deep on her cheeks now.

'Lana! He's only just lost his wife.'

Lana gave a short laugh. 'So? He's a man, isn't he?'

'He's very grieved, as we all are.'

'Yes,' said Lana, 'well, don't make yourself too much of a slave to that kid. Tell you what, you could bring her down to Marshwick some time. The twins would love it and Gerda can look after them all, she's a real treasure is our new *au pair*, eats like a horse, swears like a storm-trooper in German and is marvellous with kids.'

'Thanks,' said Maxine, 'Patsy would love that and it would give Alan's aunt Molly a break. She has trouble with her legs.'

Lana grinned. 'Don't we all, but it's nice.' Suddenly switching the subject, she said, 'Who's Cleopatra going to thread through the eye of her needle now that film star's gone back home?'

Maxine shook her head. 'She's with those awful Jameson twins today, I think. Mother wasn't too happy about the pictures in the paper of Cleo with the famous Bart Raglan, but I don't think she's said anything to her. It's not much good, is it, the way young girls are these days.'

'For Chrissake Maxine,' exploded Lana, 'you sound like a geriatric. You're a young girl yourself, dammit. For Gawd's sake chuck the knitting out the window and get yourself a feller.'

'I'm well content thank you,' said Maxine quietly.

'Listen, Maxine,' said Lana, 'don't you ever get fed up dogsbodying for mother and Cleo? They use you, you know, you're always around to organise their meals, sort out their travel tickets, arrange mother's horrible cocktail parties. You have no life of your own, Maxine.'

'I like it the way it is,' said Maxine, 'the gardening, the shopping, the accounts, helping Clarrie round the house . . . if it comes to that,' she added with an unusual touch of spirit, 'mother uses *you*, too. You do all the designing now and it all goes under the name of Hilary French.'

'Ah, but that's different,' said Lana, 'mother pays me generously for what I do for my own pleasure and she's never shown any jealousy over my designs.'

'No,' said Maxine thoughtfully, 'she treats us all very well. I wonder why we don't show more gratitude?'

'She'd be embarrassed if we did,' said Lana, 'she's very self-contained and unemotional is mother.'

Just like you, Maxine thought, and wondered why it had never occurred to her before.

Lana glanced at her jewelled watch. 'Must go soon. I'm due at the Durham's at six for cocktails.'

'Isn't Rory going with you?'

Lana shrugged. 'If he remembers and gets home in time, but he's on to selling some property to a big supermarket concern right now and what with keeping his small money-making lines going, he hasn't much time for socialising. When he does, he's a hit; the more he sends people up, the more they seem to like it, especially the women.' Lana stopped thinking of the way Rory sent Cleo up every time they met. *Was* he stringing her along for later? Were there secret messages winging between them under their snidey exchanges?

'Lana,' said Maxine worriedly, 'things *are* all right between you and Rory, aren't they?'

Lana flashed her a brilliant smile. 'Sure they are. I always said I didn't want a nine-to-five man, didn't I?'

'Yes,' said Maxine, 'he just adores the twins, doesn't he?'

'And it's mutual,' said Lana, 'but then again, they're women. Remember the first time we met Rory at the Marshalls' party? He came up to me and said, "I'm Rory Jefferson, a Scottish Cockney. I sell anything from safety pins to oil rigs and I'm going to marry you." He was married to Susie at the time, of course, an obstacle he easily removed as he removes anything that gets in his way.' She gave a short laugh. 'That's why our marriage stands a good chance. I don't get in his way.'

'Or fly flags for him,' Maxine said with a rueful smile, 'the way most women do.'

'I don't fly flags for any man,' said Lana soberly. 'Remember that, Maxine, that way lies disaster.'

When Lana and her twin daughters had gone Maxine picked up her knitting.

She thought of Alan Maxwell, the first time she'd seen him in his airline uniform, Gail's husband. Lana shouldn't have spoken of him in that cynical fashion. It hurt. Alan Maxwell was grieving for his wife.

CHAPTER FOUR

Back at the salon after her lunch with Rory, Hilary French slept off the effects of her mid-day alcohol on the pink and gold settee in her luxurious office. When she awoke she telephoned Maxine. Maxine, it seemed, was going to eat at the Maxwell house with Alan Maxwell's aunt Molly, but offered to leave her mother food in the oven as it was Clarrie's night to visit her sister. Cleo would be out too.

'Don't bother, Maxine, I'll get a light meal in a nearby restaurant.'

But after she'd showered and dressed, she

remembered that she hadn't eaten much at lunchtime and now she realised she was hungry. To hell with going to a small restaurant, she would do it in the renowned Hilary French style, she would go to the Savoy grill. Quickly she slipped out of the blouse and skirt of her suit and donned one of the several dresses she kept in a closet in her office. As she applied her makeup she thought of Rory's words. I'm forty-three. Is time slipping away from me? Is it time now to take stock? Do I need a permanent involvement? Damn Rory Jefferson—her life was no concern of his. I was crazy to have lunch with him. There *were* men in her life, friends, business contacts, with whom she enjoyed the occasional discreet amorous dalliance, but once one of them showed serious intent, Hilary French shied away. 'One night stands,' her mother had declared once, 'you should have been a man, Hilary, you have a man's metabolism.' She peered at herself in the mirror and smiled complacently. I *look* female enough and, thank God, when I'm with a man like Rory Jefferson, I *feel* extremely feminine, but what would I do with a man around all the time? The picture won't form, not yet anyway. 'Hilary dear,' she said aloud, 'let's forget Rory Jefferson and his family counsels and go eat.'

Seated at a corner table in the Savoy grill, she ordered a glass of white wine as an apéritif and, as she sipped it, she glanced around her. It was early and there were only a few people dining. As her eyes swept the restaurant they came to rest on a man who was staring at her with open interest. He was a dark man with black hair greying at the edges and, she calculated as composedly she returned his stare, in his mid-fifties. She was somewhat disconcerted when he got up and walked across to her table.

'Hilary French, I believe? I would have recognised you even if I hadn't just seen your picture in the paper, because you still look the same age as when I saw you last.'

Puzzled and a little annoyed at the man's assurance and her own slip in composure, she said coldly, 'I'm afraid you have the advantage of me. I don't know you.'

His smile momentarily took the melancholy from his eyes. 'Of course you don't remember me. You only saw me a few times and, unlike you, I've aged a lot. Luke Madden. When you knew me I was Luke Madenberg. For business reasons I changed my name.'

'Of course.' Hilary remembered him now. He was right. He had changed from a brash untidy young Jew, nephew of her boss at the sweat shop. He had become a very distinguished looking man and, by the look of his clothes and gold watch, a very prosperous one. There was an air of culture about him too. Like me, she thought, he has learned and acquired over the years. In her teens she had taken little notice of the boss's nephew on the few occasions when he visited the factory because she had been too besotted then with Graham to see another man. She smiled a welcome. Her composure had returned.

'How very nice to see you. Would you care to sit down?'

'I'd love to, but are you not waiting for someone?'

'No. I'm dining alone. And you?'

'Dining alone too. Have you ordered yet?'

'No. I'm still deciding.'

'I haven't ordered either, so may I join you?'

'I'd be delighted.'

'I'd like you to be my guest.'

'Oh no,' she protested, 'I don't . . .'

He cut in on her, smiling. 'You don't pick up men in restaurants even if the restaurant is the Savoy, but we are acquaintances after all.'

'Thank you,' she gave in graciously. 'I'd love to be your guest.'

'I was intending to get in touch with you but I didn't know until I saw that wedding picture in the paper that you were still in business. You see, I've lived in America for the past twenty years.'

'I see. What *is* your business?'

'My business *was* cosmetics, but now I'm retired. Thanks to my wife I'm a very rich man.'

Conscious of a strange feeling of disappointment Hilary said, 'Your wife is in England with you?'

'No. My wife died last August. She'd been

very ill for years.'

'I'm sorry.'

'Thank you. I miss her a lot. For years her illness gave me no freedom. Now I have my freedom and it's a little lonely. And you, your husband?'

'We divorced,' said Hilary. 'He re-married. He died recently. I went to his funeral today.'

'I'm sorry. You never re-married?'

'No.'

'Have you children?'

'Three daughters,' she said, 'all in the business with me. Lana is twenty-four, married with twin daughters and Lana designs far more brilliantly than I ever did. Maxine is twenty-two, she does the books and is general factotum, then there's the baby, Cleo, just nineteen. Cleo does a bit of everything, modelling, selling, delivering. Cleo is good at doing what she likes best, being a pretty ornament.'

'You've given your daughters lovely names,' said Luke, 'but then you would. My uncle always said you were one very exceptional lady.' With a rueful smile he added, 'You are lucky to have a family. I have no one, no friends here or relatives living. I'm quite alone.'

'Are you planning to stay in England?'

'Yes,' he replied, 'I've been pining for it for years, but my wife hated England. I'm staying here at the Savoy at present but I think I've found the place I want, Honiton Hall in the village of Ferry End on the Thames.'

'That's wonderful,' cried Hilary, surprised at the elation his reply had given her. 'You'll be near Lana, she lives in Marshwick.'

His eyes were warm on her. 'Then I shall hope to see a lot of you and your lovely daughters because, with a mother like you, they must be beautiful.'

She inclined her head. 'Thank you, sir, for the pretty compliment.'

'You must be used to them. May I say I'm surprised you didn't re-marry?'

'I've been too busy with the businesses and my daughters.'

'The girls must be a great joy to you.'

Joy, Hilary thought cynically, is hardly the right word.

'I was sorry not to come over when Uncle Rudi died, but my wife was very ill then and I couldn't leave her.'

'I miss him a lot,' said Hilary. 'He made me my first loan, you know, found me my first premises. He was wonderful to me. Just before he died we had decided to go into cosmetics together. Now I'm considering doing it on my own, but the girls . . .' She spread out her hands in a futile gesture.

'Don't,' Luke said quickly, 'you'll get more heartaches than profit, Hilary. It's a jungle. Most of my money comes from my wife's cosmetics concerns, but I'm glad to be out of the running of them now.' His voice grew gentle. 'Don't take on the hassle, Hilary, I'd hate to see lines on that lovely face.'

He used her Christian name easily and Hilary was surprised at the warmth his concern gave her. No one, except her mother, had ever given a thought to her feelings, certainly not Graham or the girls. She smiled at Luke. 'Maybe you're right, Luke. In the same way I've never ventured into the world of big fashion. Some of the really top names have approached me, but I've never wanted to join them or compete with them. My three salons are sufficient and my localised clientèle is very satisfying. To dress royalty and first ladies has never been my ambition.'

As the excellent meal progressed they talked easily together. She found herself telling him about her life with Graham and the divorce, her problems of making her way bogged down by his disapproval. She told him about each of the girls and her inability to get really close to them. Luke told Hilary about his meeting with his wife—Elsie-Jane—an heiress and head of a famous cosmetics firm. 'It wasn't her money that attracted me,' he said, 'I really loved her and I shall always be grateful to her. She moulded me in such a gentle subtle way that I never noticed I was being groomed.'

'She sounds lovely,' said Hilary.

'She was.' He sighed. 'Poor Elsie-Jane, she had so much to live for. And you, Hilary, you've worked so hard and got so little for yourself. I think that's something that must be changed.'

Hilary basked in his concern. She realised that, apart from her mother, she'd never had such a sympathetic, understanding listener. She had a host of acquaintances, but had been too busy and self-contained to make any real friends. Now today, the day of her ex-husband's funeral, two men had shown real concern for her, two men so different—Rory—hard, ruthless, compelling—Luke—quiet, steady, peaceful; already she felt the safety of his presence and the warm glow of being appreciated. Had the time come now for her to have a man of her own? To move into the passenger seat?

'You're smiling, Hilary,' Luke said, 'what are you thinking about?'

And Hilary, still smiling, said, 'Driving.'

CHAPTER FIVE

He was in his airline captain's uniform when he dashed into the house. Maxine's heart always turned over that extra little bit when she saw him in uniform. He smiled at her as he bent down to pick up Patsy, his three-year-old daughter who, already in her nightgown, was on the floor playing with a doll.

'I'll carry my brat to bed,' he said, 'then take a quick shower and change. We got held up in

Munich, that's why I'm late. Getting as bad as British Rail.'

He swung Patsy, still grasping her doll, high into the air, then lowered her so that she could kiss Maxine and his Aunt Molly 'Goodnight'.

'No bed,' protested the child, 'No bed.'

'Come on, hussy,' Alan said, grinning, 'I'm not used to women refusing me when I invite them to bed.'

Molly Waring and Maxine exchanged smiles. It was good to see Alan cheerful. Gail's illness had put lines on his face, making him look more than his thirty years. As he bore the child away, Molly Waring said to Maxine, 'It was good of you to come round here instead of letting Alan pick you up.'

'I promised Patsy I'd see her before she went to bed. I drove round although it's only a road away. I'm scared after all the muggings.'

'Yes,' said Molly. 'I'm glad you're going out to dinner tonight. It'll do you both good after the long hours you've both spent in the sick room. What a lovely dress, Maxine.'

'Thanks,' said Maxine, glancing down at her black and white dress. 'My sister, Lana, designed it for me and mother had it made up in the work room. Gail was always talking about Lana designing a dress for her when she got better,' she stopped, then asked, 'How has Patsy been today?'

'Quite good. She's asked no questions at all today.'

'That's good.'

Alan Maxwell's aunt had grown very fond of this quiet, lovely girl who'd been such a constant comfort to her nephew's dying wife and she was a little anxious now at Maxine's devotion to the child. If Alan moved away or got married again . . . ?

'You'll have more time now for your own work, Maxine,' said Molly Waring, 'it must have taken so much of your valuable time to come round here like you did.'

'Oh, I managed to fit my work in easily,' said Maxine, 'I just keep the books, work out the tax and wages. Mother has a man called Stubbs who's the full-time accountant for the three salons.' Remembering Lana's words she added with a wry smile, 'I'm just the dogsbody.'

She looked up eagerly as Alan came back into the room. He was dressed now in a smart dark grey suit, lighter grey shirt and silver tie.

'You've been quick,' commented his aunt, 'I guess that uniform's in a heap on the floor.'

He grinned at her. 'There's an angel of mercy in this house who usually picks it up for me. Anyway, I'm not flying again until day after tomorrow.' He looked directly at Maxine and her heart lifted, but then he said, 'Jock Coley and I are going to get in a day's golf if the weather holds.'

Molly was quick to see the flash of disappointment in Maxine's eyes, but Maxine said quietly, 'It'll do you good, Alan. You've had to spend so much time indoors lately.'

As he drove down the drive Alan said, 'You look a million dollars tonight, Maxine. I'm not used to driving dolls in mink. It *is* mink, isn't it?'

'Yes,' said Maxine, 'A birthday present from my mother.'

She was bursting with happiness, although she told herself it was wrong to care for Alan like this, disloyal to Gail, but, said Reason, Gail is dead, you're not taking him from Gail.

'You're very quiet, Maxine. Penny for them?'

'I was thinking of Patsy,' she lied, 'what a pretty girl she's going to be.'

'Yes,' he said soberly, 'already you can see she'll be the image of Gail, a real head-turner just like her mother.'

Maxine felt a sharp stab of jealousy and was immediately disgusted with herself.

'Thank goodness she's so young,' he said, 'she'll forget quicker than an older child. You and Aunt Moll are wonderful with her.'

'It's no hardship,' said Maxine simply, 'I love her. She's part of my life now.'

She saw his smile as they passed under a street lamp.

'You'll have one of your own one of these days.'

'Several of my own I hope,' she said quietly, 'at least three.'

'Yep,' he said, 'I imagine large families could be fun. I wouldn't know. Both Gail and I were lonely children.'

Maxine's hopes soared. Alan would like more children. She could see herself running Alan's home for him, caring for Patsy, bearing him more children, loving him to distraction. I think, she told herself, that now at this very moment I am completely happy, then he said, 'I booked seven-thirty for eight. We shall probably be sloshed by the time Len and Hazel arrive. They're always late.'

Len was Len Braddock, the doctor who'd attended Gail during her illness and Hazel was his wife. Maxine hadn't known they were coming. She'd expected a tête-à-tête dinner with Alan. Her happiness dimmed. Stupidly she repeated, 'Len and Hazel?'

'Yes. Like you, they were marvellous with Gail and I thought this dinner would be my little thank you to you all.'

'I don't need thanks,' she said bleakly, 'I did it for love. Love doesn't expect payment.'

'Maybe I put it clumsily,' he said, 'Let me put it this way. We all need a break. She won't come back and we've got to go on living.'

In the hotel bar while they waited for the Braddocks, Maxine drank martini-lemonade and Alan ordered a double scotch.

'Have to watch it,' he said, 'I'm driving.'

'I don't drink much,' said Maxine, 'so if you could trust me with your car, I'd drive home.'

'Ever driven a Porsche?'

'Yes. Mother had one last year.'

He smiled at her, gold-flecked eyes crinkling. 'In truth I could use a few drinks tonight. I feel like unwinding. Thanks, Maxine, I guess you drive like you do everything else—top efficiency.'

As he sipped his second scotch he said, 'Oh, Maxine, one of the lads in my outfit is giving a bit of a party next Wednesday at Feltham. Care to come along?'

Happiness surged over her again, then she thought, has it just occurred to him to ask me so he won't have to drink and drive? Seeing her slight hesitation he said quickly, 'If you've something better to do, don't bother. It was just a thought. Probably be a boring affair, anyway, but I haven't been out anywhere for so long that I . . .'

'I'd love to come,' she said swiftly, 'thank you, Alan.'

She would go to the salon and ask mother to choose something sensational. Mother had such a flair for knowing what suited people. When the Braddocks arrived Alan was on his third scotch and Maxine was still drinking her original martini-lemonade. Len Braddock was a large, red-faced man, more like a butcher than a doctor, with a booming voice and a store of risqué jokes at which his wife laughed dutifully. Maxine had never liked him at her mother's cocktail parties, but changed her mind about him when she saw him tending Gail and then his caring and gentleness had amazed her. His wife, too, had pottered in and out of the Maxwell house with books and delicacies for Gail, telling her all the tit-bits of local gossip. Tonight the Braddocks carefully avoided any talk of Gail. Maxine told them how Lana had suggested that she should take Patsy down to Marshwick to visit with the twins. 'If she wouldn't be homesick,' Maxine said, looking at Alan.

'Oh, Patsy wouldn't be homesick,' said Alan, 'She's an adaptable little kid and it would give Molly a break. Great idea.' He smiled directly at Maxine and the smile sent a thrill coursing through her. The whisky and the wine he was freely imbibing had put a flush on his face and his hair was a little awry. Maxine thought of him getting up in the morning, his hair rumpled, sleep in his eyes, a faint stubble showing the need to shave. She'd seen him like that one morning in the early stages of Gail's illness. He was sleeping late because he'd been on a night run and he'd come down to the kitchen for coffee. Maxine thought now, that was the moment when I first knew I loved him.

'You're looking all serious, Maxine,' said Alan, 'have some more wine.'

Laughingly she stopped him pouring more wine into her glass.

'No, Alan, remember I'm driving.'

'We guys sure know how to pick 'em, Alan,' said the doctor, 'Hazel here's got her shuvver's hat on, too.'

Len Braddock's remark somehow gave Maxine the feeling of being Alan's girl and she gave herself up to the enjoyment of the evening, laughing at Len's jokes, answering his wife's trivia, all the time feasting her eyes on Alan's face. When at last they were on their way home Alan said, 'You drive like a feller, Maxine, spot on. I can really relax with *you*.'

They were almost home when it happened. They were on the main road above the residential area known as the High Road—a road that called for extreme caution because of its sharp bend that, in the past, had caused many accidents. Maxine slowed to round it carefully, keeping well over to the left, when headlights blazed suddenly right in front of them. With immediate reaction she swung the Porsche up on to the empty pavement coming to a halt at the base of a lamp post whilst the offending car hurtled by. Alan and Maxine, jerked forward in their seat belts, looked at each other in the light of the street lamp.

'Christ!' said Alan. 'Christ!' He put an arm round her, 'Oh, love.'

Maxine was trembling. 'I'm sorry, Alan, sorry.'

'Sorry?' He kissed her lightly on the cheek and released her. 'Maxine, you were bloody magnificent. That maniac could have killed us and himself too. You're some gal, Maxine, some very special gutsy gal.'

CHAPTER SIX

Not for Rory Jefferson a swanky office shining with chrome or a thwarted model for a secretary. Rory's Scottish origin taught him the foolishness of unnecessary expense. He needed no fancy trappings to conduct his wheelings and dealings and he knew that if he had a sexy secretary he'd probably end up in bed with her and then it would cost him and business would go out the window. The two rooms he used as offices were part of a warehouse he owned in south London. In the one he used himself there were two armchairs and a drinks cabinet—the only concessions to comfort. The other office was manned almost continually by Joe Wallis, Rory's manager, secretary, errand boy, personal assistant and friend. Rory and Joe had been to school together, they'd fought together, had their first smokes and drinks together, had their first woman at the same time, all these things before they left school. Joe was not tall and handsome like Rory. He was a short solid-looking man with a shock of red hair. He had a quick temper and a ready fist and his admiration of Rory amounted almost to worship. Married and divorced, Joe was quite content now with one night stands. He knew he'd never have the luck to get a bird like Rory's Lana.

Rory was bawling now into the telephone, his feet up on his desk.

'Listen, you nurk, we could have a bloody bonanza with those teddy bears. *After* Christmas they'll be bloody dead ducks when everyone's skint.' He listened a while then he said, 'Yeh, you do that. Get orf yer fat ass and get round there with 'em *allez tout* whatsit, and those other petrol stations on the South Circular, see if they're sold out and, if they are, bung some more in pronto. Foul this up and it's the last bloody deal you do with *me*.' He slammed the 'phone down and shifted his long legs from the desk. He thumbed through an indexed book and dialled a number. The frown had disappeared, he was smiling now.

'Mrs French please,' he said crisply, 'it's Rory Jefferson, her son-in-law.' He waited, then his frown came back as he said, 'Listen carefully, darlin', tell her it's the best buy in velvet and brocade she'll ever see, but if she's busy with a customer, I'll offer it elsewhere. It's no skin off *my* nose. Just tell her that, darlin'.'

He put his feet back up on the desk and waited. Then, with a smug smile, he said softly, 'Hi there, Boadicea, got the spikes stickin' out of our chariot wheels today, have we? All right, all right, if *you're* too busy for social chit-chat, so am I. Lana tells me you're still taking orders for winter evening dresses. Well, I have this brocade and velvet the like of which hasn't been seen around since Henry the Eighth dressed Ann Boleyn in it before the chop-chop. Lana said you'd jump at it.' He listened a while, then he said, 'OK Lana will tie up the details when she goes to the salon tomorrow and, just for the record, mother-in-law, I enjoyed our lunch the other day.'

Grinning, he put the receiver down and picked up his indexed book again. He was thumbing through it when Joe poked his head round the door.

'Call for yer on line two. Shall I put it through?'

'Who is it?'

Joe grinned. 'Miss Brixton Nineteen-fourteen—Midge Mahoney.'

'Midge? What's *she* want?'

'Dunno,' Joe said, 'said it was very urgent.'

Midge Mahoney, the sister of Rory's ex-wife, Susie, was the last person Rory wanted to talk to.

'Mebbe she wants a character reference fer Will,' said Joe, 'I heard he collected another D & D last week.' Another one Rory had no time for, Midge's Irish husband, Will Mahoney, who'd been booked several times for being drunk and disorderly. These people had no place in Rory's present life-style.

'She should pay someone to push his silly face in. Never had an ounce of sense between 'em, her and Suse. Better put her through I suppose.'

'Rory?'

'Yep.'

'Rory, it's about Suse.'

'What about Suse?'

'She's in right bloody stoomp, Rory.' The girl's raw cockney tones grated. Rory thought of Lana and her cool, upmarket voice and suddenly he was filled with desire for her. He'd like to go home right now and take her to bed.

He dragged himself out of his sexual fantasy and asked wearily 'What's the silly cow done now?'

'Council's dunnin' 'er fer the rent. Say they'll chuck 'er out if she don't pay.'

'Well, she's married to Ron Potter now. The rent's *his* pigeon.'

'He's gone up north, she says, to find work. Suse don't know where he is.'

'I told the stupid cow not to marry him,' said Rory. 'Everyone knows what the Potters are like, the old feller and the boys, in and out of stir like they were on a shuttle run. I said to her "Live with him if you like, but don't tell me and you'll still get your alimony, but marry him and it stops," but the silly cow married him, didn't she?'

'Yeh well,' said Midge, 'she said she wanted to be respectable, so you'd respect her like.'

Rory gave a hard laugh. 'I wouldn't respect anyone who shacked up with one of the Potters, wedding ring or not. Anyway, there's nothing I can do. She's Ron Potter's responsibility now.'

There was a whine in Midge's voice as she

said, 'You didn't used to be so hard, Rory. Livin' in nobs' alley hasn't 'arf made you change, you and yer fifty quid voice an' all. Anyway, it's not just the rent, there's worse. Suse is preggers and soon she'll have to leave her job.'

'Stupid bitch,' said Rory in disgust, 'no one has to have kids these days if they don't want 'em.'

'Well, you know Suse.'

'Yeh,' he said wearily, 'I know Suse. Where does she work? What's her job?'

'She works nights washin' up at the Greasy Spoon.'

'What and where is the Greasy Spoon for Chrissake?'

'It's a Greek Restaurant down Beckley Street called the Grecian Moon. Everyone calls it the Greasy Spoon.' Her voice took on a sneer. 'I forgot, your caff's the Savoy now I s'pose. You wouldn't know any more about places like the Greasy Spoon.' He made no answer, then, not sneering now, she said, 'It's a lousy place for Suse to work but she couldn't get nothin' else, got no skills, Rory, see?'

'She didn't have to work,' said Rory shortly, 'Her alimony was sufficient.'

'Yeh, well, it's done now, en't it,' said Midge. Her voice grew desperate. 'Rory, I'm beggin' you, will you go round and see her, please? She was that depressed when I seen her this mornin', I'm scared she may do somethin' daft, somethin' . . . her voice trailed away. Rory thought she was crying.

'OK,' he said roughly, 'leave it to me. I'll see what I can do.'

'Oh, thanks, Rory, thanks a million. I got to go now before the boss comes back. I knew you wouldn't let 'er down. Ask Rory, I told 'er, but she said No, I'm not going to ask Rory.'

As he climbed the stairs of the high rise Council building to Susie's flat on the third floor he thanked his lucky stars he'd had the sense and the drive to get out of this sleazy world. Everything about it revolted him, kids bawling, raucous music, toys lying around, empty crisp packets blowing around, women gossiping in doorways. Once they were his kind of people. No way would they ever be again. He was shocked when Susie opened the door to him. She was dressed in a dark, shapeless woollen skirt, a jumper and a cardigan with two buttons off and her legs were bare, her feet encased in tatty fleecy slippers. She was still pretty but she looked a slut. Her hair was straight and plastered down over her head. It looked greasy. At one time Susie had taken great pride in her hair. As yet her body showed no signs of pregnancy.

'Well, Suse, what's this I hear about you being broke?'

After the first gasp of surprise at seeing him, Susie said nothing, simply stood and stared at him. Conscious of the interested looks of two women further along the balcony, he said, 'Don't you think you'd better ask me in?'

'Yeh. Yeh, course.' She stood aside for him to enter. 'Come in the kitchen, it's warmer in there.'

He looked with distaste at the dirty dishes piled in the sink. Susie had always been dirty and untidy in the home. They'd had many rows about it. In fact, three months after marrying her Rory realised that his marriage was the first real foolishness of his life. He vowed that it would be his last.

'You like a cuppa, Rory?'

'No thanks, Suse.'

'A drink then? I got some rum. Ron left half a bottle.' She gave a little laugh. 'He didn't know where I hid it, or it wouldn't be here now.'

'No drink thanks, Suse. Where's he gone?'

She spread out her hands in a futile gesture. 'Dunno really. Said he was goin' to find Jake Underwood, a mate of his what keeps a bettin' shop in Huddersfield. Said Jake would find him a job, then he'd send me some money, then if the job was OK he'd send fer me.'

'Does he know you're pregnant?'

'Yeh. That's why he went.'

Rory shook his head sadly. 'Oh, Suse, what made you marry him? You know what the Potter family is like, always nipping in and out of the slammer.'

'He was good to me at first,' said Susie,

'always bringing me little presents.' Wistfully she added, 'brought me that lovely green vase, he did.'

Rory looked at the thick glass vase which stood on the kitchen table with faded artificial flowers stuffed into it and he thought of the fine glassware in his own home and Lana's tasteful flower arrangements.

'Hardly yer Waterford crystal,' he said, 'more yer early Woolworths I'd say. Anyway, he probably nicked it off a stall in the market.'

'Yeh, mebbee.' She sighed heavily and sat down on a stool by the sink.

'How much do you owe for rent?'

She indicated a letter on the table. He took it and read it. It was from the Council stating that if the sum of £400 odd pounds was not paid by a certain date, eviction proceedings would be commenced.

'Struth, Suse!' he demanded, 'how'd you let it go on like this?'

She shook her head. 'Dunno really. I thought Ron was payin' it and he says he thought I was.'

'Did he have any money when he went north?'

'Only what I give him. What was left of me wages.'

'Christ! You'd never come top for brains, would you?' He put the letter in his pocket. 'Don't worry about this. I'll send them a cheque when I get back to the office.' He drew out his wallet and extracted five twenty-pound notes which he put down on the table. 'That'll help get a few things for yourself.'

She started to cry then, softly, hopelessly.

'Now Suse,' he said gently, 'stop that. It's bad for you. You're out of the wood now and if that bleeder's gone for good, we'll have to see what can be done. Don't you worry now, there's a good girl.'

She looked at him through tear-drenched eyes. 'You're a lovely man, Rory. How I envy that wife of yours, she oughter go down on 'er knees every night to say thanks fer you.'

Rory guffawed. 'I can just see Lana doing that, like I can see Ron Potter being the next Prime Minister.' He chuckled. 'Come to think of it, though, he might make a good one. He's got all the necessaries.'

Susie got up from her stool and held out her arms. 'Rory, would you, just this once, make love to me?'

'No, Susie,' he said gently. 'It wouldn't do, love. You're Ron Potter's wife now. It wouldn't be right for me to do that to you with another man's seed inside you.'

Her arms dropped to her side. She gave a great sigh. 'Ron would never know. I certainly wouldn't tell 'im and, anyway, it's you I love, Rory, it's always bin you.' Her eyes pleaded with him. 'Couldn't we, just this one last time?'

'No, Suse. We had fun once, but it's over now. You're married to Potter and expecting his child. I'm married to Lana and I've got two kids. We've both started new lives, don't let's mess them up.' He turned to the door. 'I'll send off a cheque for the rent today, that's a promise.'

'I know you will,' she said dully, 'you always do what you say. Goodbye, Rory, thanks fer comin'. I'll be OK now. I can manage.'

'Right, you know where I am if you want me. Take care.' He attempted a grin and nodded at her belly. 'But you don't need to take care now, do you? Stable door's already open.'

More women, some in slippers and curlers, were at their doors as he left Susie's flat. The old grapevine still functions, he thought. They eyed him curiously. Cooking smells, fish, onions, stale cabbage wafted out on to the balcony. He breathed in the cold winter air thankfully as he strode away from the building. He'd left his car several streets away where it would be safe from vandals. He thanked God for Lana as he drove away from his former life.

CHAPTER SEVEN

That night as Rory turned into his driveway he saw Cleo's red Toyota parked outside the front door. My day for stupid females, he thought. Lana was the one woman he wanted right now. 'So, Cleo, my hot potato,' he said silently, 'get your free-for-all butt out of here fast.'

As he climbed the front steps he blew a raspberry at the holly wreath on the door. He hated the thing. Wreaths were macabre he told Lana, but she insisted on putting one on the door every Christmas. Inside the house he listened, but could hear no voices from the sitting room. He shrugged out of his sheepskin jacket and dropped it, with his briefcase, on the oak settle in the hall alongside Cleo's scented fur jacket. He opened the sitting room door to find only Cleo in the room, a glass of pale liquid in her hand. She's like a doll, Rory thought, a pretty, evil, empty doll, brittle as fine china and so easy to break. She passed her tongue over her lips and drew in her breath before she said softly, 'Lana's out so I helped myself. Shall I pour you one?'

'No thanks. I'll get my own.' He moved past her to the cabinet and picked up a bottle of scotch.

'Where's Lana?'

'Six-o-clock cocktailing with the Durhams so Gerda says. Gerda's bathing the twins and putting them to bed.'

Rory frowned, remembering. 'If you're not back in time, I shall go to the Durhams alone,' Lana had said this morning.

'It was clever of Lana to get a fat plain *au pair* like Gerda,' said Cleo. 'She can leave you alone with her with an easy mind.' She moved closer to him, drowning him in her musky perfume. He poured his scotch and moved away. Cleo laughed. 'We're quite alone, Rory, does it bother you being alone with your young adoring sister-in-law?'

'Yes, it does,' he said, 'I was looking forward to a quiet drink with my wife. I'd completely forgotten the bloody cocktail party. Anyway, what brings *you* here?'

Cleo indicated a folder on a chair. 'Mother wants Lana to have a look at Lady Crosby's notes before she comes up to the salon tomorrow.' She devoured him with her hot eyes, loving the fine lines of his face, the flinty eyes, the strong firm mouth. How could a man like this be satisfied with a cold, haughty bitch like Lana?

'Are you going to wait for Lana?' asked Rory.

'Well,' said Cleo, 'I can stay a wee while and keep you company, brother-in-law. P'raps you'd like to mix me another teeny vodka-dry martini and we can have a drink together.'

'You can pour it yourself, sweet seductress,' he said, putting down his glass. 'I'm going up to see the twins.'

Cleo's low laughter followed him as he moved to the door. 'Why not, Rory?' she asked softly, 'why not?'

With what he thought was consummate acting he looked at her with mocking eyes, 'Don't you know?'

'No,' she said eagerly, 'tell me, Rory, tell me.'

'When you grow up,' he said curtly as he closed the door. He chuckled to himself as he mounted the stairs. Paul Newman couldn't have put on a better act. Another round in Cleo's game. Know what happens when you tangle with the big boys, darlin', you go down, down, down.

He stayed playing with his small daughters, Juliet and Corinne, until Gerda stated firmly that it was time for bed. As he disentangled himself from their clutches he heard the closing of the front door. He waited on the stairs until he heard Cleo's car drive away. He was on his second scotch when Lana came in. She sniffed. 'Smells like a prostitute's bedroom.' She spotted the folder on the chair. 'Cleo's been here.'

'She was here when I got in having mixed herself a drink.'

'When did she leave?'

'I dunno. I had one drink and then went upstairs to the twins.'

Lana sank into a chair. 'Mix me a good strong martini. Those Freddie mixed were made with cheap vermouth.'

As he got up to do her drink he said, 'Nice of you to be here to greet me after a hard day's grafting.'

She grinned. 'You had Cleo. I mean that in the nicest possible way, of course.'

'I didn't want Cleo.' He handed her the drink. 'I wanted you.'

Lana slipped her shoes off as she took the glass.

'Maybe you'd like me to sit here with a lighted lamp in the window to guide you home.'

'Yes, I would.'

'As Long as He Needs Me is Shirley Bassey's song,' Lana said. 'Not mine.' Eyeing him over the rim of her glass she asked, 'What did Cleo say?'

'That your mother wants you to look over the notes before going to the salon tomorrow.'

'I'm designing the old trout three evening gowns,' said Lana. 'By the way, is mother taking the brocade and velvet?'

'Yes.'

'Good. I'll do them in that. Lady Crosby can afford it.' She sipped her drink appreciatively. 'You make a good martini. God, I'm bushed. I don't feel like making supper tonight. Let's tell Gerda and go out. Let's go over to Shoppenhanger's Manor, they have lovely log fires over there.'

'On one condition,' said Rory, sipping his third scotch.

'What's that?'

'That we use taxis. I'm not risking drinking and driving.'

'OK.'

'There is one other condition.'

'What's that?'

'That you come to bed with me first.'

Her lovely eyes widened in surprise. Then soberly she said, 'Was it Cleo turned you on?'

'No it wasn't,' he said quietly, 'I've been wanting you all day, since precisely ten a.m. if you must know.' He held out his hand and she took it, rising to stand in front of him. 'I'll never stop wanting you, Lana,' he said, 'ever.'

*　　*　　*

Rory saw them first as he guided Lana to a table in the lounge. Hilary's beautifully coiffured head was close to the man's as they were laughing softly at some shared joke. Rory had a momentary urge to make an excuse and withdraw, but by that time Lana had seen them too as she sat down.

'Good Lord! There's mother. Who's that she's with?'

Hilary looked up then and saw them. Instantly she was on her feet murmuring something to the man, who rose too. Rory advanced to meet them.

'What a pleasant surprise,' said Hilary, looking beyond Rory to her daughter. 'Who would have expected you to be here?'

'Who would have expected *you*?' replied Rory, 'you've got a lot further to come than we have.'

'We wanted to get out of town,' said Hilary.

The three of them turned to Lana at the

table, Hilary suddenly anxious that Lana might resent her presence here, but Lana was looking at Luke Madden with undisguised interest. Lana was feeling on top of the world now from the martinis and the love-making. Looking at her, Hilary thought, Lana has the look of a woman who has recently had very satisfactory loving. Rory caught her eye and his gently mocking smile told her she was right. Damn the man, Hilary thought, for his uncanny understanding.

As the introductions were made Hilary knew at once that Luke and Rory would like each other, they were two of a kind.

As Luke took Lana's hand he said, 'Well, now I've met one lovely daughter, one down, two to go. Is yours a private party, or may we all dine together?'

'Sounds great,' said Rory, looking at Lana, who nodded imperceptibly. 'Be our guests.'

'Be mine,' said Luke. 'After all, we were here first.'

Rory inclined his head. 'So be it, provided we can return the compliment in the future.'

'That I shall look forward to,' said Luke.

He was an easy conversationalist and was clearly delighted with his reception into Hilary's family. He told them about the old days of his uncle's sweat shop in the East End, his own life in the States, his late wife's cosmetics business. 'I love American martinis, American cars, American friendliness but, above all, I love England. I shall never leave again except maybe for a holiday.'

As the evening progressed, Lana grew pleasantly tipsy and Hilary hadn't been so happy for years. She realised suddenly that in the short time since meeting Luke at the Savoy, she'd come to think of him as belonging. After all, he had no living relatives and all his former friends had disappeared. He sought her company constantly, although he had never yet made any move towards her other than friendliness.

When Lana heard that Luke was buying Honiton Hall in the village of Ferry End, she was wildly enthusiastic.

'That's a gorgeous house, really baronial, and very close to us.'

'Your mother is helping me choose my furnishings,' said Luke and very soon he was having earnest discussions with Rory whose sources of supply would be of great help in obtaining the best at the lowest prices.

With a tiny mocking smile Lana said, 'Well, Luke, with the taste of Madame Elegance and the backyard tactics of the robber baron, you should have the most luxurious cost price house in England. You'll be squire of the village with the peasants tipping their caps at you.'

Luke smiled back at her. 'And bussing the maidens on the village green.'

'Maybe you can get Luke on the regatta committee, Lana,' said Rory.

'No, thanks,' said Luke in mock horror. 'I know nothing about boats. I'm just a cockney boy up from the smoke, the only sport I ever indulged in was the occasional punch-up in the Rose & Crown on a Saturday night, in my very young days, of course.'

On the way home in the back of the taxi Lana's head drooped on to Rory's shoulder. It was a bright clear night with a full moon and, as he glanced down at her, the trees threw dancing shadows across her face.

'It was a lovely, lovely, lovely evening. I simply adored every little, single, tiny minute of it.'

'Yes,' he said, grinning, 'it was great.'

'I like Luke. Do *you* like Luke, Rory? But then, of course you do. He's one of us, isn't he?' She gave a tipsy giggle. 'Shoots plastic ducks and smashes a few faces in down the ol' Rose and Crown. Olé!' She moved and snuggled her face into his neck. 'Say, maybe I'm gonna have a real daddy at last. Won't that be fun, Rory, a daddy jus' like my husband, giving me lovely presents and shooting harmless little ducks whizzing up and down on the water, poor little ducks, never . . . never did anyone any harm.' She lifted her head for a second. 'I like ducks. Our nurse used to take us to the park to feed them.' Her head dropped back to his shoulder again. 'Dear little ducks skimming over the water, whoosh!'

Rory chuckled. 'You, my darling Mrs

Jefferson, are beautifully, deliciously tight. Know that? And you'll have a hell of a hangover tomorrow.'

She nuzzled deeper into his neck and waved one arm airily. 'Tomorrow and tomorrow and tomorrow. Somebody said that. Who was it?'

'You,' he said, 'just now.'

She giggled again and moved to kiss his cheek.

'You're so clever,' she gurgled, 'so de-de-devious an' crazy an' clever. I like you better than Father Christmas, much better than Father Christmas,' and then she fell asleep.

Rory cradled her in his arms and leant back more comfortably on the seat—one very satisfied man.

CHAPTER EIGHT

Maxine knew that her model dress was the envy of most women at the party, but the knowledge gave her little pleasure. She felt out of place amongst these light-hearted, slick-talking airline people who all seemed to know each other. Maxine hated her mother's cocktail parties too, but at least at those she had things to do looking after the guests. Here she sat quietly with a middle-aged couple, parents of the hostess—Felice Brandon—a former airline stewardess. From their conversation Maxine gathered that Felice was Bill Brandon's second wife, Bill Brandon was Alan's friend, they both worked for the same airline.

'You've got to admire Fellie,' the woman said, 'she manages pretty well considering Bill has to pay out so much to his first wife and those kids.' She glanced at Maxine's ringless hands. 'You're not married then, Miss . . . ?'

'No,' said Maxine, 'I'm Maxine French. I came with Alan Maxwell. I was a friend of his wife's.'

'Ah yes.' Both the man and the woman warmed to her. 'You're the angel of mercy Bill told us about, said you were marvellous with that poor dying girl and her little daughter.'

'She's lovely,' Maxine said, 'little Patsy.'

'What will happen to her now.'

'Alan's aunt is looking after her.' Maxine wanted to escape before these people started speculating on Alan's future plans. She was still upset over her mother's remarks to her at breakfast this morning.

'Don't get too attached to that child, Maxine. Alan Maxwell might move or get married again and then you'd get hurt.'

Couldn't they see that if Alan *did* re-marry, it might be to the girl who, in recent months, had played such a big part in his life and his daughter's? His spontaneous words, 'Oh, love!' on the night they almost had an accident had echoed in her ears ever since and she could still feel the warmth of his arms in that one brief embrace. That showed that he cared, but he was still naturally grieving for Gail and would be for a long time, although he didn't appear to be grieving tonight. But then, Maxine told herself, Alan wasn't the sort of man to intrude his grief on a party. He was standing with others round the piano where a young flier, Tony Tempest, whom everyone called 'Windy', was thumping out the tune and singing 'My Way' to the accompaniment of bawdy suggestions from his audience. Faces were flushed, glasses drained rapidly and everyone called everyone else 'Sweet' or 'Darling'. Alan had one arm rested carelessly on the shoulder of a young brunette who answered to the name of Bobby. Maxine thought she was the girl friend of the pianist but she had been too confused at Alan's introductions to be able to sort people out.

The couple Maxine had been talking to excused themselves, got up and moved away. As Maxine rose too, a blonde in a white pants suit drifted up to her. 'Hi, sweet, I'm Peg Simms. You're Maxine French, aren't you? I just adore the things in your mother's salon, but they're far too pricey for me.' Then she said, still taking in the details of Maxine's dress, 'You're not a bit how I imagined you. From the way Alan spoke of you I pictured you older, a bit like those social worker persons I suppose. One never thinks of them wearing model dresses, does one?' Without waiting for Maxine to reply, she went on to talk about Gail before her illness.

'Some of the gang wrote her off as snooty, but I don't think she was snooty, just a bit reserved, but it was plain to see she adored Alan.'

'And he, her,' replied Maxine shortly.

'Yes, of course, goes without saying, doesn't it? Poor cow, much good it does her now,' and the blonde added, 'See yah,' and drifted away.

'Your date doesn't look too happy, son,' said Bill Brandon, moving up beside Alan at the piano. 'She's looking a bit lost. Don't think this is quite her scene.'

Alan glanced over at Maxine who was talking now to a young lad of about fifteen, someone's kid brother who looked as ill at ease as Maxine. Alan had been drinking fast and had quite forgotten Maxine. 'I'll rescue her in a minute. She's a good kid is our Maxine. She couldn't have done more for poor Gail if they'd been sisters.'

'And for you?' asked Bill with a grin.

'I don't foul my own doorstep, mate.'

'No,' said Bill, 'there's no need, is there?' He was thinking of all the accommodating stewardesses and holiday makers who'd given Alan Maxwell his bedroom comforts in European hotels during Gail's illness when she could no longer perform the functions of a wife. No one blamed the poor sod.

'I know it's early days,' said Bill, 'but, in time,

laddie, you'll maybe marry again. After all, you're a young man and there's little Patsy and . . .'

Alan cut him short. 'No, Bill. I want to be free again. I realise now I married too young. Oh, I know I was deeply in love with Gail and, had she lived, I suppose I'd have had no regrets, but now I know, deep down, that I wasn't ready for permanence and kids. I want fun, freedom, quiet tête-à-tête dinners uninterrupted by dashes upstairs to change nappies. I want to stay in bed with my bird all day if I feel like it, no kid scrambling into bed with us at the crack of dawn, take off for a dirty weekend, Paris, Berlin, Monte, give parties, raise a bit of hell now and then.'

'I know what you mean,' said Bill, 'but, in time, it palls.'

'So it palls.' Alan gave a mirthless laugh. 'I just want to try it, mate, and then if it palls, well, say, oh hell, can I have another drink? I don't have to watch it tonight, Maxine will drive home. She's one hell of a driver is our Maxine.'

'Is that why you brought her?'

'No. I s'pose I'm trying to repay her for what she did for Gail and for what she's still doing for Patsy. She really adores that child.'

Bill, five years older than Alan, felt sympathy with Alan's needs, but he felt deeper sympathy for Maxine who was so obviously crazy about him. Was Alan really so blind that he couldn't see?

On the way home, Maxine driving, Alan said, 'You didn't really enjoy that party tonight, did you, Maxine?'

'Yes I did. It was very nice.'

He gave a low chuckle. 'What a sweet, polite little fibber you are. Maxine, you don't have to pretend with me. I thought it was pretty deadly too. If it hadn't been for hurting old Bill I wouldn't have gone.'

And then I wouldn't have been here with you, Maxine thought. 'Well I quite liked it,' she said firmly. 'The food was gorgeous.'

They were on the fateful High Road now. Alan turned to her.

'Scared of the bend, Maxine?'

'No,' replied Maxine, 'I've driven round it several times since that night.' That wonderful night when you showed that you cared.

'The Council should do something about it,' said Alan, 'it's a bloody death-trap.'

Although, at the time, Maxine had been frightened, she had loved that near-accident because it had thrown herself and Alan into a brief, exciting intimacy. Tonight Alan was formal again. On the way to the party he had talked about taking Patsy to see Father Christmas at a West End store. Now, on the way home, he had talked about the toy car he was buying for Patsy.

'Alan,' said Maxine as she drove the Porsche swiftly, expertly home, 'would you and your aunt and Patsy care to spend Christmas Day with us? Mother would be very pleased if you'd come. She'd like to meet you. All my family will be there and also a friend from mother's teenage days, a Mr Luke Madden who has come from the States to live in England. Lana's twins will be there too so Patsy will have someone to play with.'

'Sounds great,' said Alan, 'don't think I'm on duty over Christmas. Thanks, Maxine, we'd love to come.'

Maxine drove on. She was happy again. In spite of the pretty, racy women at the party, she, Maxine, was Alan's date and she would be with him again on Christmas Day. After that she could afford to wait.

'It's a lovely night,' she said. 'I just love Christmas.'

CHAPTER NINE

'I'm glad Christmas is over,' Hilary said to Maris, her chief sales girl, 'now we can concentrate on work.' Fat lot of concentrating you'll be doing, Maris thought, with that Mr Madden ringing you up all hours of the day and you dashing out every time he beckons. Most unlike the Hilary French we all know and love. Still, madam had been better tempered since Luke Madden had come on the scene.

When Maris had gone Hilary sat awhile thinking. She was haunted by the desolate look on Maxine's face the day before Christmas Eve as she turned from the 'phone. 'Alan's not coming to us on Christmas Day, Mother, he's volunteered to do duty for another pilot whose wife has just had a baby. Then he's going off the day after Boxing Day for a ten days' ski-ing holiday with his friend, Jock Coley.'

'Do him good,' Hilary had said briskly, pretending not to see the despair in Maxine's eyes. 'Anyway, the aunt and the child can still come to us for Christmas, can't they?' Hilary was so afraid that Maxine would get hurt, but every time she attempted the subject Maxine would shut up like a clam. At twenty-two Maxine should be out on dates instead of exchanging recipes with Alan Maxwell's aunt and knitting garments for his child and taking the child out instead of consorting with young people of her own age. She sighed and turned her thoughts to pleasanter things. Apart from the quiet of Maxine, it had been a good Christmas, Luke and Rory taking over and making the usually disapproving Clarrie their devoted slave.

Cleo had been Hilary's chief worry, having said on Christmas Eve, 'What's this old fart like then? Shall we be expected to sit at his knee while he talks to you,' she put on a mock quavery voice, 'Do you remember, Hilary, when we were young?'

'He is *not*, as you so elegantly put it, an old fart,' Hilary had said angrily, 'and I shall expect you to be civil to him. It's a pity you were out when he came into the salon or you'd have seen for yourself that he's a handsome charming man. And, listen Cleo, I don't want the Jameson twins round here at Christmas either.'

'They've gone to Venice,' said Cleo, which explained why Cleo was spending Christmas at home. Anyhow, to Hilary's great relief, Cleo had shown an almost angelic sweetness towards Luke over Christmas and the pose endured in spite of the odd goading, snidey remark from Rory. Rory's attitude to Cleo puzzled Hilary. Was he attracted to the girl or was he putting her on? She was sure that Cleo thought the former, but Rory was a ruthless one, not the kind to be brought down by a woman, even one as pretty and sexually inviting as Cleo. Cleo loved money and men in that order. Maybe, Hilary thought, she's playing up to Luke thinking that if I marry him, she'll be the number-one spoilt, pampered daughter. If I marry Luke. Did all these attentions he was paying her mean eventual marriage? Luke was not the sort of man to ask a woman to live with him without. All the signs were there, theatre tickets, quiet dinners, flowers, perfumes, presents; and he sought her company at every turn, not even trying to make other friends. And now there was his house—Honiton Hall. Almost everything that was going in it had been selected by Hilary, even the pictures. The house had become a family affair. Lana was working with Hilary on suggestions for the interior decoration and Rory was a tower of strength in the finding and buying of furniture and effects. Now Hilary had to leave it all for ten days to make her customary New Year visit to the Paris salon where she planned the year's programme, visited valued customers, wined and dined with designers, suppliers and the like. Ten action-packed exciting days that, until now, had been a bright spot in her life.

'I shall miss you,' Luke had said.

'I shall miss you, too.' She'd almost said, 'Come with me,' and, as if guessing her thoughts, he said, 'I'd come over for a day or two, but you'll be busy and I have so much going on here with the house being available so much sooner than I thought. I daren't leave town even for a day.'

'The time will soon pass,' Hilary said, 'and then . . .' what then? she asked herself now. Will I have to decide if I'm brave enough to give up my little empire and start a new life? Only one person can make that decision, me. The kind of life Luke was planning at Honiton Hall would be all-consuming. Would Hilary French, the East End machinist, be content to opt out of her success and become lady of the manor? If you love him, Hilary, yes. Do I love him? Does he love *me*? Hilary sighed once more, pulled her notepad towards her and carried on with making plans for Paris.

CHAPTER TEN

'Should be a good year for us,' Rory said, shaking a few flakes of watery snow from his driving gloves before tossing them on to a chair. 'I feel it in me water.'

Joe Wallis looked up from the typewriter on which he had been studiously pounding. Rory grinned at him. 'You go much faster on that machine, Joe, you'll need a bucket of water thrown over it.'

'That's what I gotta talk to you about,' said Joe, leaning back in his chair. 'Now you're expanding so fast I can't cope with the typing, and sending it out is a bind. We've got to get someone in, Rory, there's room enough in my office fer another desk and,' he smiled sheepishly, 'I thought mebbe we could get one of them posh 'lectric memory typewriters.'

'Oh yes,' said Rory, 'and a posh nymphomaniac to operate it, I suppose?'

'That's not what I had in mind.'

'Oh, what *do* you have in mind?'

'Well,' said Joe. 'Y'know Mabe Filey down the Arches pub?'

'Yeh, I know Mabe.'

'Well, Mabe's sister, Ruby, she's just turned sixty and she lost her job last week when

Macey's went to the wall. She'd bin old man Macey's secretary for over thirty years and he's given 'er a smashin' reference. She's a real worker Mabe says.'

'Knowing old Macey she'd have to be,' Rory said. 'Well, you're the office manager, Joseph my man, engage the old bird by all means. We may have to get bigger premises soon as well.'

'Right,' said Joe. 'Oh, I almost forgot, you gotta ring Midge Mahoney, says it's very urgent.' He handed Rory a piece of paper. 'That's the number.'

'Oh Christ!' said Rory disgustedly, 'Not that shower again. What's up now? Is it Suse again?'

'Dunno. Said somethin' about she gotta warn you.'

'Got to warn me about what?'

Before Joe could reply the 'phone on his desk rang. He picked it up.

'Jefferson Incorporated,' he said cautiously, then he put a hand over the mouthpiece. 'It's 'er again, Midge.'

With a shrug and a sigh Rory said. 'OK. Shove it through to my office.' He strode through into his own office and shed his sheepskin jacket. The 'phone buzzed and he lifted the receiver.

'Yes Midge, what is it now, for Chrissake?'

'It's Suse, Rory, she's bin beat up real bad. They took her to Bankside General. They let me stay with her while she was unconscious and when she came to, she asked fer you. Then she said "Tell Rory ter look out fer Ron". Ron could be after you, Rory.'

'Ron Potter after *me*? You gotta be joking. If he beat her up why haven't the Old Bill got him?'

'Seems she told 'em 'er husband was away from home and an unknown intruder attacked her, but I know it was Potter because Ma Flagg who lives in Number 23 rang and told me, but Ma Flagg won't tell the police because she's scared of them Potters on account of her Jimmy. I am, too. Christ, Rory, what a bleedin' mess! Will you nip in and see Suse, Rory, during tonight's visitin' hours? She's out of intensive care now; please.'

'OK,' said Rory, 'but you and Suse don't half know how to cock things up.'

He slammed down the 'phone, then picked it up again and dialled his home number. He told Lana that something had come up and that he wouldn't be in to dinner. Lana accepted this without comment, as always.

'What are you going to do with yourself today?' he asked her. She had been in bed this morning when he'd left.

'Making a porn movie with Freddie Durham this morning,' she replied, 'and playing snowballs with the vicar this afternoon. God, Rory, don't tell me you've started making noises like a suburban husband at last?'

Rory chuckled, his irritation at Midge and Susie momentarily erased by the sound of his wife's cool cultured voice.

'OK. When I get back I'll shoot bloody Durham and stick a broom up the vicar's snowman's arse and I'll give you two guesses what I'll do to *you*.'

'I can hardly wait,' said Lana. 'Have fun.'

'And you, sweet, be happy.'

He was smiling as he replaced the 'phone but his fury rose to boiling point that evening when he handed his flowers to a hovering nurse and sat down beside Susie's bed. The nurse explained to him that the screens were round Susie's bed just during the visiting period so that her bruises wouldn't be exposed to visitors on the ward.

Both Susie's eyes were black and there was a livid bruise down one cheek. Her lips were cut and swollen and one arm was set in plaster.

She turned towards him, the pain of moving showing in her wobbly smile. Through her swollen lips she gasped. 'Rory.'

'Don't try to talk too much, Suse.'

'I gotta. It don't hurt quite so much as it did. They'll all go in time, they say, all the cuts an' bruises.'

'He must be made to pay for this.'

'No, Rory, no. It'd all come out and your wife would be upset. 'Sides,' she managed a feeble smile, 'with '*is* record it wouldn't do 'im too much good neither, would it?'

'Bastard! Where is he now?'

She spoke slowly, with difficulty. ''e come

back with money, but not fer me.' Her eyes closed with weariness and pain. 'Shacked up with Reenie Watts down the Silver Bullet. Them women on my landing what saw you come that day, they told him, found out 'bout the rent, he went mad.' Her blurry voice tailed away. Rory reached for her good hand and held it in his. She opened her eyes and smiled at him. 'Love you, Rory, always will.'

'The baby?' he queried gently.

She moved her head from side to side. 'No baby. Not now. Good thing, jus' me now, Rory, jus' me.'

He was filled with pity for her. All right, she was stupid, but she didn't deserve this.

'When you come out, Suse . . .'

'Go to Slough, help Jess.'

Rory had met Susie's aunt Jessie once, a sleazy woman running a pub near Slough.

'Good,' he said. 'I'll let you have some money.'

Wearily she shook her head. 'No need. Midge rang Jess. Jess gonna . . .' she drew her hand from his and put it under the sheet. 'Tired, Rory, so tired.'

He got up and pushed aside the screens. 'Nurse,' he said, 'she seems to have lost consciousness.'

The nurse came and looked down at the poor battered face.

'She's just sleeping. She's been heavily sedated and talking has probably tired her out.'

'She's OK though?'

'Yes. She's doing fine but I think it would be as well for you to go now. She'll sleep for hours.'

On his way out he stopped at the Sister's office and knocked on the door.

'About Mrs Potter.'

The sister looked at him curiously. 'You're not Mr Potter?'

'No. I was married to her once, long time ago. Will she be all right?'

'Yes, eventually. She's got a strong constitution. She lost the baby of course.'

'Yes, so she said.'

'Mr Potter hasn't been to see her,' the Sister said. 'Have you any idea where he is?'

'No,' said Rory. 'Last I heard was he'd gone up north.'

'Well, whoever did this to her certainly made a good job of it,' said the Sister, 'and for what? As I understand it, there was nothing of any value in her flat. May I ask how you heard of the incident?'

'Her sister rang me this morning.'

'Oh yes, Mrs Mahoney. She was with her when they brought her in.'

'If there's anything I can do,' said Rory.

The Sister was studying him, taking in the expensive gear, her eyes openly curious, faintly hostile.

'You're not a relative, Mr . . .'

'Jefferson. I know, but if there's anything,

here's my card.'

She waved it away. 'There won't be, Mr Jefferson,' she said coolly. 'If anything is required we shall contact the relatives and, as I understand it, her sister, Mrs Mahoney, is her only available next of kin. Good evening to you Mr . . .' she paused, 'Jefferson.'

Rory grinned to himself as he left the office. Got starch in their bodies as well as their uniform, a bloke could break his fingers on it.

Before he left the hospital he 'phoned Joe at his flat from a public call box.

'How bad is she?' Joe asked.

'Bad. Do you know Reenie Watts at the Silver Bullet?'

'Who doesn't?' replied Joe.

'Ron Potter does apparently. Just where is the Silver Bullet, Joe?'

'It's that boozer on Market Alley,' said Joe, 'bin renamed, you know it, used to be the Dog and Duck. Say, Rory . . .'

'What?'

'Like me to come with you?'

'No thanks, mate, this I have to do on my own, probably with one arm tied behind my back.'

'Them Potters don't fight by the rules,' said Joe, 'watch 'em fer sly ones like a cutter. The only time they ever do any real fightin' is when they can muster four to one.'

'I'll be careful,' said Rory, 'and so will Ron Potter be after this.'

There were only a few people in the saloon bar of the Silver Bullet when Rory entered. Ron Potter, dressed in a loud check suit, a pink bow at his neck, was lounging half on a stool in the corner, a glass in one hand, the other hand idly stroking the bosom of a young brunette leaning over the bar towards him. As Rory strode across the bar Ron Potter's eyes dilated. He put down the glass and took his hand from the girl's bosom. Then he settled himself more firmly on the stool and uttered a shaky laugh.

'Why, if it isn't the man come to pay the rent.' He turned to a short fat man who'd come to stand at the girl's side behind the bar.

'Meet Mr Money Bags, Reenie, Algy, the guy who screws my missus when I'm away and pays 'er rent. Ask him . . .'

He got no further. Rory grabbed his lapels and jerked him off the stool. No one else in the bar made a move or a sound, they just sat or stood in silent fascination as Rory rammed his fist into Ron Potter's face between the eyes, knocking him to the floor. As the man groaned and made to get up, Rory jabbed his foot viciously into his gut.

'Now for the kid she lost,' he snarled, and delivered another savage kick at his victim's groin. The silence of the spectators was broken now by a single unanimous gasp, then even while Potter was shrieking and sobbing with pain, Rory bent and kicked him again in the face. 'And that's a bonus for Suse,' he said.

Blood was streaming down Ron Potter's face. He seemed to have lost consciousness. Rory became aware then of the onlookers, he looked around, but no one stepped forward to challenge him. The girl had made no sound, now with curious precision she lifted the flap, came round and bent down over Potter sprawled on the floor.

'The name's Jefferson,' Rory said. 'Rory Jefferson, but somehow I don't think he'll want you to call the police. When he comes to, tell him the Casualty department at Bankside General would like to talk to him.' Rory paused, then he said, 'Seems someone who looked like him beat up his wife.'

For a second no one moved or spoke, then excited babblings broke out but no one made a move against Rory. The man on the floor opened his bloodied eyes and groaned. Rory turned and walked slowly to the door.

He felt so good that he ate an expensive gourmet meal at a French restaurant in the West End after cleaning up first in the men's room. His knuckles hurt, but it was a good hurt. He hadn't felt so exhilarated for years. He finished off his meal with a large brandy. On the way out he rang Joe from the 'phone at reception.

'Joe.'

'Rory.' Joe's anxiety showed in his utterance of that one word.

'Potter's fixed.'

'And you?'

'OK. Found a superb restaurant with a gorgeous receptionist. You must try it some time.' He smiled at the girl who'd let him use the 'phone. 'Tell you about it tomorrow, Joe. Bye.' He replaced the receiver, smiled again at the girl and then he went home.

CHAPTER ELEVEN

Hilary took a taxi from the airport straight to the salon. She and Lana had arranged to go through some of Lana's designs with a rich, important customer at 11 o'clock. It was now ten. Paris hadn't been so much fun this year. The men who wined and dined Hilary seemed foppish after Luke, and there had been none of the amorous dalliance that was usually a part of her Paris visits. She had spent each night in her own bed and in spite of a packed schedule, the time had dragged. Does this mean I'm really in love? she asked herself.

When she arrived at the salon Cleo was draping a flimsy stole over a model dress. Cleo had a talent for pairing up the most unlikely colours with startlingly exciting effect, but only when she was in the mood. Mostly she was not.

'Hello Mother,' Cleo said demurely, 'had a good trip?'

'Yes thank you, Cleo. How have things been

here?'

'Things have been very good here,' replied Cleo. With a tiny smile she added, 'Maxine's been in every day to check. Something should be done about Maxine, Mother, she'd win hands down the spinster of the year contest.'

'Yes, well, I haven't time to discuss Maxine now,' said Hilary, 'Lana should be in soon. Mrs Stacpoole is due in at eleven, see that she's taken in to me at once, we have to give *her* the full treatment.'

Hilary waited for Cleo's usual jealous comments on the wealth of the Stacpooles, but Cleo had gone back to re-arranging the stole. 'Oh Mother.' She spoke over her shoulder without looking round. 'Luke rang. Maris told him what time you were due in and he's calling back.'

'Right. Thanks.' As she sat down at her desk Hilary found that she was in a fever of excitement like a young girl with her first love. She hoped Luke would ring before Lana came in because she found herself suddenly shy of talking to him under Lana's cool, cynical gaze. Over Christmas she had noticed with some embarrassment that Lana would occasionally look from her mother to Luke with quizzical eyes. At that moment the telephone on the desk emitted its discreet purr and she lifted it up.

'Hilary!'

'Luke!'

‘I’ve missed you. Had a good trip?’

‘Yes thanks. Most satisfactory, but I’ve missed *you*, too.’

He gave a self-conscious kind of laugh. Hilary guessed he was nervous, too.

‘You’ll be organising that house-warming party for me sooner than you thought, Hilary. Thanks to Rory the house is coming on by leaps and bounds. Guess what, we’re going to convert the billiards room into a swimming pool, but not until the Spring.’

‘I’m very impressed. And Rory knows just where to find the best swimming pools?’

‘That’s right.’

‘Well, at least a swimming pool can’t fall off the back of an aircraft or lorry, can it?’

‘I think you’re not quite fair to Rory,’ he said, laughing.

‘Nonsense. He loves it, his swashbuckling pirate image. He works on it.’ Her voice softened uncharacteristically. ‘All men are babies at heart.’

‘And all women want to mother them.’

‘I don’t think mothering is what women have in mind for Rory,’ said Hilary, ‘but why are we talking about Rory? Tell me more about the house.’

‘Not now. Can you dine with me tonight?’ His voice dropped and he gave a little cough before he said, ‘I have something very important to discuss with you.’

This was it. The die was cast now. Keeping

her voice steady she said, 'I'd love to dine with you. Where and what time?'

'Trevi's in Brady Court. It's a delightful little Italian place I went to the other night. I'd come and pick you up, but I'm due at the Pomona for cocktails at six. Would 7.30 suit you? Brady Court is just off . . .'

'I know Trevi's,' Hilary interrupted him, 'we sometimes have family birthday dinners there. I'll be there at 7.30. I have to go now, Luke, I have a customer due in any minute.'

As she replaced the 'phone Hilary wondered how Luke had found Trevi's. Had it been recommended to him by someone? And who was he having cocktails with tonight? He had no friends in England, but then she thought, his lawyer. He'd said what a nice man the lawyer was, going out of his way to give help and advice.

Hilary found it hard to concentrate on work. As she went through Lana's designs with Lana and Doreen Stacpoole incoherent thoughts jumbled through her brain. Maybe Lana would take over the salons with Cleo and Maxine, gradually of course. What will happen to my lovely North London house? I've spent so much money and thought on it that I'd hate to sell it. Maybe Maxine and Cleo would keep it on, but what would be the point of keeping it on? I should never go back to it. My home for the future would be Honiton Hall in the country, away from London where I've lived all my life. Problems and possibilities chased each other through her mind all day.

Luke, when he greeted her that evening, took her hands and said simply, 'Hilary, you look more wonderful each time I see you. No one would believe you had three grown-up daughters.'

'Then let's forget my daughters,' she said, linking her arm through his as he led her down the steps into the small dining room.

'Would you like a drink before we order?'

'Love one,' said Hilary, 'I've had a hectic day and I had to get up early this morning to catch my plane.'

Luke was instantly concerned. 'I'd forgotten that. If you're tired . . .'

'No, I'm not tired,' she said, reassuring him, 'not in the least, just in dire need of a stiff drink, that's all.'

He relaxed. With a rueful smile he said, 'I'm drinking plain tonic, I'm afraid. I've been drinking martinis rather fast. I must ease up.'

She looked at him anxiously. 'You are rather pale, Luke, are you all right?'

'Just a bit of a headache, too many drinks too fast. I suppose I was trying to get Dutch courage.'

'Am I so frightening?'

'No. You're lovely.'

'What is it, then?' she asked gently, 'that you have to tell me?'

The moment has come, she thought, there

will be no going back now.

'Wait till we're mellow on our brandies?' he pleaded.

Hilary smiled at his fears. 'All right,' she said, 'There's plenty of time.'

After all, she and Luke were not exactly young lovers. Throughout dinner they talked with forced lightness about Paris, about Luke's new house, the salons, like two acquaintances trying to keep the conversation flowing. The ease had temporarily left their relationship, but when at last they were sipping their brandies the old intimacy returned.

'Hilary my dear.'

She gave him a gentle smile. 'The moment of truth?'

'Yes,' he said quietly, 'the moment of truth, Hilary . . .' his words were halting, he ran his tongue over his lips, 'Hilary, I'd never thought to marry again when Elsie-Jane died.' He paused, then he said 'I loved her so much, I didn't think I could fall in love again.' He looked away from her questioning eyes. 'It just happened.'

'Yes,' she said, 'I think I understand.'

'Hilary . . .'

'Yes, Luke?'

She noticed again his pallor and the gravity in his eyes. Surely he should look happier if he were a man in love?

'Hilary,' he said hoarsely, 'this will probably come as a great shock to you, but you see,

Hilary, I want to marry Cleo.'

CHAPTER TWELVE

'So there you have it,' said Hilary. 'Send in the clowns.'

Lana sat in her mother's office, head in hands. 'I still can't believe it. The man must be stark, raving mad.'

'At least it's solved one problem for me.'

Lana looked up. 'What's that?'

'What to do with my house if I married. I'd hate to give it up.'

Lana looked at her curiously. 'You're not upset?'

'Surprised. I don't know if I'm upset.'

'But Luke was yours.'

'I must admit I thought so, but Luke doesn't know that. I deserve an Oscar for my performance when he told me.' Hilary smiled thinly. 'He said he realised he was filling a father need for poor little Cleo, she'd obviously given him some spiel about missing her daddy.'

'Little shit!' said Lana. 'Luke Madden and Cleo. It's disgusting.'

'When a woman of over fifty marries a boy of nineteen,' said Hilary, 'the world jeers, but when a *man* of over fifty marries a girl of nineteen, the world admires and envies. It's not considered disgusting.'

'She must have swung into action the moment you left for Paris,' said Lana.

'Poor Luke,' said Hilary, 'He doesn't know what's hit him.'

Lana snorted. 'Serves him right, the stupid, randy old fool.'

'I don't think of him that way,' said Hilary, 'Luke is one of nature's gentlemen and he's in love with youth. Is that so wrong? Don't forget he was married for years to a very sick woman.'

'I shan't go to the wedding.'

'Oh yes you will, Lana,' Hilary said with unusual vehemence, 'we shall all go to the wedding bright and smiling in our head-turning Hilary French gear and the media will love it. Do you want to give Cleo what she's craving for, the satisfaction of having dropped a bomb on us? From me she was expecting shock, jealousy, criticism. Instead I behaved as if it were of little consequence and asked her what she'd like me to do to prepare for the wedding. She was almost in shock at the way I took her news. I hope you'll react in the same way.'

Lana nodded. 'You're right, of course. When's the wedding to be?'

'Madly soon—mid-February and she wants you to design her wedding gown. She'll be here in a minute to discuss it with you. She's out with Luke at the moment on a shopping spree.'

'Like hell I will,' said Lana.

'Please Lana,' said Hilary, 'design the bloody dress. I don't often ask you for anything. Do this for me.'

'Oh shit! All right, but I know what I'd rather design for the little cow. How did Maxine take the news?'

'Calmly,' said Hilary, 'sometimes lately I could shake Maxine, she's so taken up with that Alan Maxwell that she might be in another world. This afternoon she's driving his little girl to a kid's party somewhere.'

'Does Alan Maxwell take Maxine out?'

'She's been out with him a couple of times, but mostly I believe he's playing golf when he's not flying. Maxine spends an awful lot of time with his aunt and the child. It worries me.' She stopped as Cleo's voice was heard in the showroom.

'Well,' said Lana as, without knocking, Cleo swung into her mother's office. 'The child bride cometh.'

'Coffee, Cleo?' asked Hilary calmly, indicating the percolator at her side.

'No thanks, Mother. I've just had tea with Luke.'

Lana gave an elaborate yawn and covered her mouth with a white be-ringed hand. 'Mother's been telling me the glad news.'

For a second Cleo looked disconcerted. Mother's right, Lana thought, she wanted to make impact and she's failed.

'Weren't you surprised?'

'Not really. Nothing you do would surprise me and at least he's a vast improvement on

Bunny Jameson. I *am* surprised at Luke, though, saddling himself with an IQ like yours.'

Cleo was angry. This was not going the way she'd planned. 'It's not my IQ he's interested in,' she snapped.

'Spare us the porn,' said Lana lazily, 'I hear you want me to design your dress. Not white, surely? Wouldn't a dirty grey be more appropriate?'

'I love you too, Lana,' said Cleo with a forced smile.

Instead of being the heroine of a drama, Cleo was being relegated to the rôle of just another customer of the Hilary French salon. Mother and Lana, she decided, were cold, unfeeling women. Cleo had thought that Mother would be upset at Luke's defection, even heart-broken, but obviously she cared nothing for him other than as a friend. Suddenly Cleo felt curiously flat.

'This dress,' Lana demanded with a show of impatience. 'Tell me your ideas and then I can go. I have a date in an hour.'

'Oh,' Cleo came out of her depressing thoughts. 'I thought oyster satin, very heavy satin, and I want it sort of draped at the front, looped up, kind of, to just below the knee, the rest of the dress, long.'

Lana got the picture and secretly applauded it. On Cleo's slight figure it would look stunning, but she wouldn't let Cleo see her approval too quickly.

'If you can't see it,' Cleo said, 'I'm sure other designers would.'

'Oh, I can see it all right,' said Lana, 'and I'll do it, let you have some sketches.' She smiled sweetly at her younger sister. 'Funny, when I think of bridal gowns, my mind goes automatically to virgins. Silly, isn't it?'

'Very,' said Cleo, smiling sweetly back, 'and terribly down-market. Look what Luke bought me today.' She thrust her wrist under Lana's nose. 'See, isn't it divine? Every digit of the watch is a diamond.'

Lana afforded the watch a brief glance. 'Flashy. I saw an Arab wearing one of those in Harrods the other day. Just another gimmick.'

'Ah, but such an expensive gimmick. You'll never guess how much it cost.'

'I'm not really interested,' said Lana.

Cleo grinned. 'Could you, perhaps, be jealous?'

'No,' said Lana, unperturbed, 'because if I mentioned it to Rory, he'd get me one and I don't want one. Mother says Luke's giving you an American Firebird for a wedding present. If you drive that like you drive your Toyota, Luke'll soon be a merry widower again, prey to some other little gold-digger. What will you do with the Toyota? Give it to Oxfam?'

But Cleo was not heeding. Rory, how would he feel about her marrying Luke? 'Grow up,' he'd said to her once. Well, now she was grown up. Would Rory understand this was just one more step towards the ultimate?

'Rory is the only male in the family,' she said, 'he'll have to give me away.' She smiled dreamily. 'Rory and I, we shall make a lovely couple walking down the aisle.'

A sudden jealous fury seized Lana but she said languidly, 'If he agrees to do it. He has an aversion to snakes and piranhas.'

A slow smile lifted Cleo's pretty mouth. 'Scared of me, is he? That's fine for starters.'

'Don't be so melodramatic, Cleo,' said Hilary curtly, 'Rory's not clay to be manipulated by a stupid girl, if Luke is; Rory's a man.' Maliciously she added, 'there are dozens of girls around prettier than you. What makes you think you're so special? You're acting like a character out of the old Bette Davis films. Get into reality, girl, before you make yourself a laughing stock.'

This was a speech so uncharacteristic of Hilary that both girls stared at her in open amazement, then Cleo burst into tears and ran from the office.

Hilary spread out her hands with an apologetic smile. 'Sorry.'

'You were great,' said Lana with a warmth she'd never shown to her mother before. 'Thanks for calling Rory a man.'

Hilary looked at her steadily. 'Well, he is, isn't he? And he's yours. See that you keep him.'

Both Cleo and Lana had left the salon when

Rory arrived. Hilary looked up from her papers.

'Lana left about half an hour ago.'

Without being invited he dropped into the chair opposite her.

'I know. I've seen her. Just dropped in to say I'm sorry.'

Hilary looked at him coldly. 'Sorry for what?'

'Another soddin' son-in-law?' It was a question.

'I can cope. At least this one's civilised.'

He grinned. 'Don't bank on it. Know what me old grandad used to say?'

'No, but I'm sure you're going to tell me.'

'Them what's quiet what's hot, that's what me old grandad used to say, smart old geyser, me old grandad. They say I take after him.'

'I don't doubt it,' said Hilary. 'Rory, do you know anything about cosmetics?'

He looked surprised, then he said, 'I know where I can get some . . .'

She cut in on him. 'I'm not talking about stuff falling out of the hold of airliners. I'm talking about starting in cosmetics and costume jewellery, the Hilary French beauty salon.'

'I thought you weren't interested.'

'I've been reconsidering since I was approached again in Paris.'

'But I thought Luke advised against it.'

She smiled faintly. 'Recent events have made me question Luke's judgment.'

'Yeh,' he said, grinning, 'I know what you mean.'

'If I take it on and get problems, would you be willing to give me the benefit of your undoubted business expertise? And if I should need advice, would you give me counsel?'

'I'd be honoured to help, mother-in-law,' he said seriously, 'at any time and in any way.'

'Thanks. I'm going to have a bash even though Luke says it's a jungle.'

Rory gave her a lop-sided smile, 'I can do a good line in bush hats and safari boots.'

She returned his smile. 'I'm sure you can and the wild animals just might be fun.'

'Anything that moves I can hit. I was the crack shot of Camberwell Fair.'

'So you'll ride shotgun for me if I need it?'

He put his hand on his heart.

'All the way, lady, all the way down the trail.'

CHAPTER THIRTEEN

'This is the nicest room in the house,' said Cleo softly, 'the master bedroom.' She stood looking at the ornate four-poster bed with its heavy gold and crimson drapes. She passed her tongue slowly over her lips. 'How wonderful to make love inside those secret curtains. Oh, Luke, we can pretend we're guilty lovers, that I'm the maidservant being seduced by the master of the house.'

Luke winced. 'We don't need to play games, my dearest, and are you sure you want to keep that bed? Isn't it a trifle theatrical?'

'No, it's lovely.' Cleo smiled. Luke, at her insistence, had got that old-fashioned bed through Rory. Had Rory envisaged himself inside those curtains with her? Had he grown hard thinking of her in there playing with her middle-aged husband? She was conscious of the moisture between her thighs as she moved over to Luke and let him cradle her in her arms.

'Careful! Don't crush Teddy.'

He smiled indulgently as she lifted her teddy bear clear of their embrace.

'You won't mind Teddy sleping with us every night? He's slept with me since I was three.'

'Lucky Teddy.'

Cleo pouted. 'He'll probably be jealous.'

'Just so long as he doesn't attack me.'

'Don't make fun of him, Luke, Teddy's very sensitive.'

'Sorry.' He kissed the top of her head. 'I wouldn't do anything to hurt you *or* Teddy.'

She wriggled out of his embrace and turned her head away.

'Luke, there's something I must tell you.'

'Yes darling? What?'

'Can we go and sit on the bed while I tell you?'

Luke hesitated. He feared the intimacy of those curtains until he could take his delights inside them legally. He owed that much at least to his very dear Hilary. 'Can't you tell me here darling?'

'No. It's a secret so it's got to be in a very special place.'

She took his hand and led him to the bed. She placed the teddy-bear at the foot of the bed and slipped off her shoes.

'Take your shoes off, Luke.'

'Darling, there's no need.'

'But I want you to lie down and hold me while I tell you my secret.'

With an inward groan he slipped off his shoes and lay down beside her on the bed. She laughed softly and pressed up against him. Gently he moved her a little away.

'Don't tempt me, darling. You must know how badly I want you.'

'Then take me, darling, that's what I have to tell you. I'm not a virgin.'

At her softly spoken words a sharp pain seared across Luke's temples. So far today he'd been free of his headaches, but now his head began to throb again. Reason said young people these days start sex before they leave school, why should Cleo be any different? But he wanted to weep for the lost innocence of her, his lovely darling baby.

'It's not what you're thinking, Luke.' She raised herself and looked down at him as he lay there, her breath warm on his face. 'It was rape, Luke, rape.'

Pity mingled with lust as he listened to her softly spoken recital.

'I was upset, Luke, because mother didn't care how I got home from that party. Coral's grandfather offered to drive me home. I was only fifteen. He was an old man. He . . . I was so scared, Luke, so frightened, then, after the first shock, I began to like it.'

She covered her face with her hands. 'That made me so ashamed, Luke, liking it, so ashamed.'

'Oh God!' said Luke, easing her gently down on the bed. 'What did your mother do about it?'

'I didn't tell her. It would have been no use, Luke. All mother was interested in was the business. That's why my father left. She gave us food, clothes and a good education and she thought that was enough.'

'But your sisters?' Luke queried, 'couldn't you have confided in your sisters?'

'No. Lana was married and away at the time. Besides, Lana's hard like mother. Maxine was in hospital. I cleansed myself as best I could and prayed that I wouldn't have a baby.'

'Oh God!' said Luke. He gathered her to him. 'My poor, poor little sweetheart.'

Cleo had always been able to cry to order. She made sure there were tears on her cheeks now as she pressed her face to his. 'Luke,' she cried, 'darling, so I can forget, make love to me please, show me that you don't hate me.'

'Hate you, darling?' he said, his voice hoarse with lust, 'how could I hate you? I adore you, every lovely inch of you. You're my darling baby bride.'

'Then take me, darling, take me.'

Pain raged and pounded through his temples as he removed his clothes and hers and as he thrust himself into her, Cleo cried aloud in ecstasy and, in her heart, she whispered, 'Rory.'

* * *

When Cleo left Luke she drove straight to the Jamesons' flat. Only Polly was there, in her studio, painting.

'You should lock the door. Anyone could walk in.'

Without looking round Polly said, 'That's what I'm hoping.'

'You might be raped and murdered.'

'He wouldn't have time to murder me, he'd be too busy on the second and third rapes.'

'Where's Bunny?'

'Birmingham.' Maliciously Polly added, 'He's got a girl there, a real raver.'

Cleo hugged her teddy-bear to her stomach. 'I don't care. Poll, you *will* be my bridesmaid, won't you?'

'No,' said Polly, standing back to regard her work. 'Neither shall I attend the wedding. Weddings nauseate me.'

'Me too,' said Cleo, sinking on to a chair.

'Not there,' snapped Polly, 'you're in my light.'

'Sorry.' Cleo got up holding Teddy by one arm. 'Oh, Poll, I'm so bloody depressed.'

'There's some hash in my bag, help yourself.'

'Thanks, but I better not. I've got to see Lana about bridesmaids' dresses. Now there'll be only one, Maxine. Lana has refused to be my matron-of-honour. Oh God, I'm so depressed.'

'You should be flying,' said Polly, 'marrying all that money and think of the kicks lifting your mother's boyfriend. Wish I could do the same but Martha keeps hers under their stones.'

'There weren't any kicks,' said Cleo glumly, 'she didn't care and Lana's treating it all as a huge joke. Oh God, I sometimes wish I'd never been born.'

'Sometimes so do I,' retorted Polly, 'and today's one of those times. Get out Cleo, will you and let me work? I have to earn a crust, you know, I've got no poor sod waiting to fly *me* to the moon.'

'Only Teddy loves me,' Cleo said as she mooched to the door, Teddy cradled in her arms. In the doorway she paused and her eyes lit feverishly. 'There's one man none of you know about. He wants me and one day he's going to love me and then you'll be surprised, all of you.' And Lana most of all, she said silently, 'see if she thinks it's a fun thing then.'

*   *   *

When Maxine was sure the invitations would have been received, she went eagerly to the Maxwell house. If Alan should be on duty on the wedding day, he would surely be able to swop with someone. Alan himself let her into the house. To her amazement and joy he picked her up and swung her round as if she were a child. 'Congratulate me, Maxine, I've been chosen to play cricket for the airline.'

'Great!' She smiled back at him as he set her down. His nearness in those first few seconds had been intoxicating. Her heart thumped with joy.

'If it snows here in February,' he said, 'I shan't give a damn.'

Apprehension stealing over her she asked carefully, 'Where are you playing this cricket then?'

'South Africa. Three whole weeks in the glorious sun. I leave on the 14th.'

The world started to tumble again.

'Then you won't be here for Cleo's wedding?'

'Ah, the wedding.' Reluctantly he sobered. 'No, I'm afraid I won't be here for the wedding. Keep an eye on Molly and Patsy for me, Maxine, will you, whilst I'm away?'

She raised her head and looked at him with despondent eyes.

'You know I will, Alan,' she said levelly, 'you

didn't have to ask.'

He tucked her hand under her arm. 'Thanks Maxine. Come on in and have a drink. Three weeks in the sun. Just imagine.'

Just one more disappointment, Maxine thought drearily, when he comes back the winter will be nearly over.

'When you come back,' she said, 'it will be almost spring.'

His eyes clouded briefly. 'And Gail's daffodils,' he said, 'how quickly the times goes by.'

CHAPTER FOURTEEN

Things had been hectic in the salon this morning but now Hilary had time to relax and read Luke's last letter.

'It's been such a long honeymoon,' (was there a hint of regret in those words?) 'but it is coming to an end and we should be back second week in April. Paris, Hong Kong and now Singapore. My dearest girl is entranced by these glamorous places, but I shall be glad to get home, the varying climates don't suit me. My headaches seem to get worse and the giddy spells more frequent. I think I shall have to see a quack when we get home. Cleo is so popular with everyone and so full of life that it's difficult for her to understand when I can't keep up the pace. I shut my eyes and picture Honiton Hall in the spring. The agent said it was famous for its masses of snowdrops, crocuses and daffodils. It will be glorious. I think of you, Hilary my dear, enjoying the sight of them on your inspections. I really am deeply grateful to you for keeping an eye on the property and my staff. I guess they think it's money for jam at the moment, but just wait until my darling girl gets back and sets them on their toes.'

And she will, Hilary thought, if I know my darling girl. She read on.

'I suppose the snowdrops and crocuses will be over by the time we get home but there will be the daffodils. I can't wait to take up residence and really enjoy that lovely English house. It's what I dreamed of whilst I was living in the States and I thought it would never be mine.'

'Poor Luke,' said Hilary silently, 'when you proposed to Cleo you didn't bargain on being dragged halfway round the globe. Does it serve you right, I wonder? Strangely, she thought, I have no feelings of spite or jealousy—just anxiety for a very dear friend. Poor Luke. Cleo will never settle in Honiton Hall. 'Cleo is at the moment,' Luke wrote, 'out on a sight-seeing tour with some film people who are making commercials here. I decided not to go with them. I get tired so quickly.'

Hilary frowned. Luke was only in his early

fifties. Surely he shouldn't get all that tired and have headaches and dizzy spells? Immediately he gets home, she decided, I'll make him see a doctor. Then she checked herself. Luke was Cleo's responsibility now, but somehow she couldn't see Cleo caring for Luke's needs. 'Cleo takes her teddy-bear with her everywhere,' Luke wrote, 'everyone is most amused. They talk to him as if he's a person and Cleo loves it. It's a game I'm not good at, I'm afraid.' That blasted teddy-bear, Hilary thought. How many times in the past has she used that toy to shelter behind, when she was little; 'Teddy made me do it.' Some people were amused then. Luke went on to say he hoped Hilary would undertake the organisation of his house-warming party as Cleo would find it too big a task, Cleo says Maxine is good at that sort of thing so no doubt she will help you.

It won't be Cleo's kind of party, Hilary thought. She hoped Cleo wouldn't insist on inviting the Jameson twins. Luke ended his remarks about the party by saying, 'Of course, Hilary, you and Maxine invite any of your own friends you think might like to come.' Hilary knew who Maxine would ask.

* * *

The daffodils were, in fact, in their full golden glory when Luke and his bride eventually moved into Honiton Hall after a further brief extension of their honeymoon in Tangier. Luke was so happy to be home. He was so proud of the beautiful mansion, elegantly and luxuriously furnished. The grounds and lawns were immaculate, sloping down to a creek which was an off-stream of the main river. Beyond the creek a line of trees bounded the river.

Luke's cup of happiness was brimming over. His passionate pretty wife was a constant joy and if she seemed a little bored at present, he told himself, it was probably the aftermath of an exciting holiday. She had been so loving and enthusiastic on their honeymoon and he had so much enjoyed her pleasure at all the exciting places they visited, but all Luke wanted now was to settle down with her in their new home, to entertain and be entertained. He would devote himself to his darling's happiness. She was such a child with her quick changes of mood, baby tears changing to joy for some pretty bauble. He laughed when she drove off, her teddy-bear at her side, in the red Firebird he'd given her as a wedding present. When he told her to drive carefully, she just grinned and said, 'Oh Luke, it's such a super car and Teddy loves it.'

Luke reckoned that now, in his settled

routine, the giddy spells would cease and his head would be clearer. If he didn't improve, then he would see a doctor. He would register with a local doctor anyway, he decided, in case Cleo ever needed one. They had never discussed birth control. He took no precautions and, as far as he knew, neither did Cleo. His thoughts went winging, would she in time give him a child? 'Oh, Cleo,' he murmured silently, 'my love, my darling.'

*   *   *

Luke's darling was, in fact, at that moment in bed with Bunny Jameson.

'Where does the old fart think you are?'

'Shopping with Polly. Oh God, Bunny, I think I'm going crazy. It's like something out of Upstairs, Downstairs. He's so fussy I could scream sometimes and the way those crappy servants fawn over him.' Her voice rose hysterically. 'The bloody swimming pool, the bloody garden, the bloody daffodils . . .'

Bunny tickled her navel with a feather, 'What's he like in the sack?'

Cleo pushed the feather away. 'Good when he's not tired. It excites me. It feels like incest because he once belonged to my mother. It was nice taking him away from her, but . . .' she stopped, frowning.

'Real little pervert, aren't you?'

Cleo pounded the pillow. 'Oh God, how I miss London. I hate the country. It's cold and damp. Teddy hates it, too, don't you, precious?'

Bunny absently stroked the teddy-bear's ears.

'Can't you have him re-modelled so we can have sex with him?'

'Luke?'

'No, prawn, the bear.'

She pushed his hand away and cradled the teddy-bear to her breast.

'He's pure and he doesn't like being called the bear.'

Bunny gave a snort of disgust and rolled away from her to light a joint.

'I thought you, of all people, would understand,' said Cleo.

'Look,' he said, 'I don't know what you're beefing about. You can get to London in thirty minutes in that souped-up motor of yours. You've got everything, kiddo, everything.'

'No,' said Cleo. She took the joint from him, inhaled and gave it back.

'One day I shall have everything and one man.'

'And two or three or four,' said Bunny.

'No,' said Cleo, floating, 'one man and only Teddy knows his name.'

CHAPTER FIFTEEN

'The dress Maxine will be wearing tonight is really sensational,' Lana said, 'she jibbed a bit at the bare shoulder, but mother and I insisted. I designed that creation with man in mind. If Maxine doesn't land that bloody airline captain tonight, it won't be the fault of the dress.'

'Maxine's one very lovely girl,' said Rory, 'but the oomf is missing. No matter if the dress is a knock-out, if the oomf isn't there, it won't work.'

'And you're the expert, aren't you?' said Lana sweetly.

He grinned. 'I know oomf when I see it. I'm married to it.' He moved over and put one finger on his wife's right nipple as she sat, topless, at her dressing-table. 'Don't let's go to the party. Let's send Gerda out for a take-away and then after we've eaten it and cracked a bottle of bubbly, we can go to bed.'

'Don't be silly,' said Lana, 'we have to go to the party to support Luke and mother. After all, she organised it. Cleo just didn't want to know. I can't see Cleo as the chatelaine of Honiton Hall, the picture just won't form.'

'I lunched at Barbarella's the other day,' said Rory, 'and Cleo was there with those grotty Jamesons.'

Lana turned from the mirror, frowning. 'You didn't say.'

'Slipped my mind.'

'And Luke wasn't with them?'

'Good Lord, no! But I bet he paid.' Rory hesitated, then he said, 'The Jamesons were high as kites and they didn't get it out of a bottle. Cleo had that stupid teddy-bear on a chair beside her.'

'Did she see you?'

'Yes. Came over and invited me back to the Jamesons' flat with them.'

Lana tensed. 'And?'

'Hal Levison was with me.'

'And if he hadn't been?'

Rory grinned. 'If he hadn't been, I wouldn't have been lunching there. I was his guest. He's the supermarket mogul.' He moved up to her and put his arms round her, stroking her breasts. 'I don't need pale ale, sweetheart, when I can get sparkling champers on tap.'

She twisted out of his embrace. 'You'll muss my hair.'

'I was nowhere near your hair.'

'Get showered and dressed, eh? We don't want to be late.'

She watched him as he mooched through to the bathroom. If Cleo hadn't been with the Jamesons and Rory hadn't been with Hal Levison, what then? She smiled with pride and satisfaction as she slipped into her gown for the evening but silly little fears niggled at her heart.

* * *

'Hilary,' said Luke, 'you look wonderful.' He took from her the fur jacket she had shed as she crossed the hall, and gave it to the hovering butler. 'Thank you for coming early.' He raised her hands to his lips.

'You look most distinguished, Luke,' said Hilary, smiling. 'I thought I'd go straight through to the kitchens to see the caterers. Where's Cleo? Still dressing?'

His eyes clouded. 'She's still out. She went out in her car about four, said she had to see Polly Jameson but she'd be back in an hour.' He glanced at his watch. 'It's now quarter to seven and she hasn't 'phoned.'

Hilary hid her annoyance. 'Don't worry, Luke. Cleo would never win prizes for punctuality. I guess they're talking and she's lost track of the time.'

His eyes cleared. 'I expect you're right. I'll go back upstairs and get some of her things out ready.'

Before going through to the kitchens Hilary went into the library and found a telephone directory. She dialled a number and Bunny Jameson answered. 'This is Hilary French. Is Cleo there?'

A languid voice replied, 'Sure, but she's just leaving.'

'Now listen,' said Hilary, 'you tell Cleo to move her butt homewards at once and I do mean at once or she'll find herself the *ex*-Mrs Luke Madden.' She slammed the 'phone down and took herself off to the kitchens seething with anger at her youngest daughter. Poor Luke. Didn't he know disaster when he saw it?

By the time Cleo's Firebird raced up the drive Luke's headache had become almost unbearable. As he paced the bedroom floor a giddy spell overtook him and he sank down on the four-poster bed. He realised now that he would have to see a doctor. Lana lived locally. She would know of a good doctor. He would ask Lana tonight and make an appointment first thing tomorrow. He had washed down two pain-killers with a glass of water when Cleo swung into the bedroom.

'My love!' he cried, going towards her, 'I've been out of my mind with worry. Where *have* you been?'

She flounced away from him. 'To London,' she spat at him, 'to civilisation.' She turned round, tears of frustration in her lovely eyes. 'Oh God, Luke, don't you realise how I hate this place? It's dead—dead, dark and dreary, this gloomy house, those stupid musical-comedy servants. I hate it, I tell you, hate it. Why can't we have a villa or an apartment in Hollywood or somewhere exciting where there are real people, not stuffed shirts and cardigans like we get here? I've nothing in common with them, nothing.'

'But Cleo, darling . . .' His hurt eyes pleaded with her. 'This house is so beautiful, the grounds, the pool, the tennis courts, why, just think how lovely it will be in the summer.'

'But it's bloody April,' Cleo yelled at him, 'and even in the summer I won't like it.'

Defeated now, he sank down on her dressing-table stool and put his hands to his throbbing temples.

A sob in her voice, she said, 'It's nothing but a bloody morgue.'

He looked up at her despairingly. 'I didn't realise. I thought your depression was just the aftermath of an exciting holiday. I thought that you . . .' She looked like an angry child staring at him with tearful accusing eyes and the enormity of his folly flooded over him. How could he have hoped to make her happy? In a last desperate attempt he said, 'Cleo, please try, for *my* sake, we'll fill the house with your kind of people if that's what you want. Money's no problem, darling, we're very, very rich.'

Reality hit her then. Where would she be without Luke? Back on mother's payroll. The mind boggled at that. Bleak as it was, she would have to stay with Luke, for the time being anyway. After all, one day there would be Rory. 'I'd better take a bath,' she said dully, 'or I'll be late.'

In her bathroom she popped a couple of the pills Bunny had given her to see her through the party and when she rejoined Luke in the bedroom she was smiling, her eyes feverishly bright.

As always, he marvelled at her quick change

of mood, but this time he asked himself how long he could live with it. She came up and kissed him and as the towel dropped from around her waist to the floor exposing her shapely young body, his manhood swelled with desire but, at the same time, the pain in his head flared violently through the haze of the pain-killers and he felt sick.

'I'm sorry, Luke. I'll try to make you happy, really I will.'

She picked up the towel and tossed it on to the bed. Then she reached over for the teddy-bear on her pillow and hugged it to her.

'You can't come to the silly old party, Teds my precious, but mummy will come back to you as soon as she can.' She turned to face Luke, the bear clutched to her breast.

'Teddy says he thinks you look handsome in your "formals", Luke, but Teddy doesn't like living in the country any more than I do. He's going to try, though, aren't you, precious?'

She put the bear back on the bed and moved towards Luke. He took her hands and stepped back to avoid contact with her naked body.

'In the summer a holiday in Hollywood, Luke?' she coaxed.

'In the summer,' he answered wearily.

'You can have me now on the bed. Teddy won't mind.'

Luke dropped her hands and turned away. 'There isn't time. Dress now, Cleo, please.'

'You're not angry?'

'No. I'm not angry.' He smiled at her, his lovely baby girl, but there was a great heaviness in his heart.

High on the drugs Cleo, standing beside her husband, received her guests like a pretty doll programmed with the right words. Her dress was a sensation in simplicity, Grecian style with a high neck and long sleeves. Her only adornments were her wedding and engagement rings. A faint smile on her lips she graciously acknowledged the admiration of the women, the homage of the men and only when she saw Maxine did her face un-freeze. Her gaze slid from her sister's sensational black dress to the man at Maxine's side. In the same instant Alan Maxwell looked up. Their eyes locked and something blazed between them, something each had never known before. Then Maxine was murmuring introductions, but Cleo and Alan didn't need them. She was Eve holding out the apple and he was the hungry man. They had no need of words.

CHAPTER SIXTEEN

June came in with a blaze of sunshine and Hilary relaxed for the first time in weeks. What with visits to the Manchester salon and the exciting new cosmetics venture in Paris, she'd had little time to herself. Rory had come up with the proposal that she should combine the sale of high quality scarves and belts with the cosmetics, an idea she had instantly accepted. The results were already proving him right. The name—Hilary French—was now over one of the most chic salons in Paris where the pure silk scarves and jewelled belts were discreetly displayed amidst the gleaming bottles and packages of the perfumes and beauty aids. If only Maxine could be persuaded to work in the Paris salon, Hilary thought, it would open up a new world for her, but Maxine just wasn't interested.

Of her two younger daughters Hilary saw little. Maxine spent most of her spare time with Alan Maxwell's aunt and child and sometimes went on family outings with Alan, the aunt and child. Hilary had long since given up trying to warn Maxine of the folly of getting too involved.

Cleo had called in to the salon twice since her marriage for clothes. Hilary hadn't seen Luke since his house-warming party, although he had telephoned her several times with invitations which she had been unable to accept because of other commitments.

Hilary saw quite a lot of Lana and Rory, Lana in connection with her design work for the salon and Rory for business chats. Since their luncheon together on the day of Graham French's funeral, an armed truce had been declared between Hilary and Rory and although neither would admit it, they each enjoyed the stimulation of their wordy exchanges and invigorating antagonism.

Hilary, on this bright June morning, sat at her desk wondering what to do with her unusual few hours of freedom. She was about to 'phone home and invite Maxine out to lunch when she remembered that Maxine had taken Patsy Maxwell to join Lana and the twins for a day's outing on the river.

The telephone on her desk purred. 'Freedom over before it started,' she murmured as she lifted the receiver.

'Hilary, it's Luke.'

'Luke! How nice. I was just thinking of . . .'

'Hilary,' he cut in, 'she's gone.' His voice rose a shade. 'Cleo's gone.'

'Gone? Gone where?'

'Gone away,' he said, 'with Maxine's friend, Alan Maxwell. She left this morning before I got up. Because of my headaches I've been sleeping in my dressing room.'

Cleo and Alan Maxwell! Oh God, Maxine! Maxine! In spite of the heat of the day Hilary could feel a clammy chill taking over her body. Her mouth was stiff with shock.

'Hilary, are you there?'

'Yes. Shall I come down?'

'Please. There's something else I have to tell you.'

His calm scared her. What else did he have to tell her? It couldn't be worse than Cleo and

Alan Maxwell surely? Anger replaced shock as she thought of her youngest daughter conceived during a time of bitterness and suspicion in a marriage already on the rocks. 'I wish you'd never been born, greedy and destructive even as a child,' she said silently, 'you took Luke and threw him aside; how long, I wonder, before you fling this one back?'

The manservant, John Flaxman, met her on her arrival at Honiton Hall. Hilary and Flaxman had established mutual liking and respect during Hilary's visits to the Hall whilst Luke and Cleo were on honeymoon. One look at Flaxman's face now told Hilary that he knew.

'How is he?'

'Stunned I think, Mrs French, although he's behaving very calmly. He even had his breakfast as usual, toast and coffee.'

'Where is he now?'

'On the terrace.'

'I'll go to him. Oh, has he had a drink, a proper one I mean?'

'Not yet. He usually has a martini at twelve.'

Hilary glanced at her watch. 'Half-eleven. Let's break the pattern. I know I could use a drink.'

He smiled at her thinking what a pleasant contrast she was to her bitch of a daughter. If only the guv'nor had married *her*. She was pretty enough in all conscience.

'Two *double* martinis,' she said returning his smile, 'lots of gin.'

She found Luke seated on the terrace at a marble topped table. He rose to greet her, holding out his hands. She took them and motioned to him to sit.

He looks like an old man, she thought, as she sat down beside him. Could this be the smooth, smiling man who'd made himself known to her at the Savoy such a short time ago?

'The staff know,' he said. 'I told Flaxman to tell them.'

She nodded. 'Are you sure she's gone for good?'

'Yes. She took all her clothes, furs and jewellery, and,' his mouth twisted in a pained smile, 'that stupid teddy-bear. She'd never leave that.'

Flaxman came from the french windows with a tray holding two glasses.

'Will you be staying for lunch, Mrs French?'

'Yes, John, but only a very light one please, cheese and salad.'

When the man had gone Luke reached for his glass, but his hand searched the air futilely before he found it and gripped it. Just as if he were drunk, Hilary thought.

'To you, my dear. Your good health.'

She smiled twistedly. 'My family hasn't exactly been good for you, has it?'

'I love your family, Hilary, all of it.'

'Do you know where she is, Luke?'

'Not exactly. She left a note.' He took a piece of folded paper from his pocket and handed it to her.

Hilary's anger rose anew as she read Cleo's childishly formed hand.

'My very dear Luke, it wouldn't be honest to stay hear with you when I'm madely in love with another man. I love Alan Maxwell and he loves me, so we are going to live together. I don't want you to divorce me if it will upset you. I am staying in a hotel until Alan has told his aunt and can take me to his home. Don't think to badly of me Luke and thank you for all the lovly presents you have given me. I shall always think of you. Cleo.'

'Only four spelling mistakes. Maybe he's educating her, the sneaky bastard.'

She put the note down on the table.

They sat in silence for a while, then Hilary said gently, 'You had something else to tell me, Luke?'

'Yes. You're a strong woman, Hilary, or I wouldn't burden you with it. Promise me, please, that what I have to tell you, you will repeat to no one.'

Hilary looked at him steadily. 'I don't think I can promise, Luke, not if it should affect any member of my family.'

A weary smile lifted his mouth. 'It affects only one and, as it happens, not adversely.'

'Then I promise,' she said.

'I have to tell someone and you're the only one I have left now.' Again the weak smile. 'I apologise for the drama, that sounded like something straight out of Charles Dickens.' He looked at her now unsmiling, his eyes steady. 'I'm going to die, Hilary. I have a deep-seated brain tumour. I left it too late and now it's inoperable. I'm going to die.'

She just stared at him—she could find no words.

'Firstly the headaches, that's when I should have gone to a medic, although they say that probably it was too late even then. Headaches when we were on honeymoon, then giddy spells and, lately, difficulty in focusing.'

Like just now, she thought, when he was reaching for the glass.

'Maybe it's good after all that Cleo has someone to love her. It would have been terrible for her and for me if she had been here to watch me die.'

Hilary found her voice then. 'Damn Cleo to hell,' she said, 'Oh Luke, my dear, my dear. There must be something, someone . . .'

She had taken his hands and was gripping them fiercely as if wanting to make him say there *was* something that could be done. He shook his head and, with a great heaving sigh, she released them.

'And I thought that nothing could be worse than Cleo and Alan Maxwell. Are you quite sure, Luke? Isn't there even the tiniest doubt?'

'None at all.'

She reached out and took his hands, gently this time.

'I shall be with you, Luke, wherever and whenever you need me.'

'Thank you, my darling. You know . . .' he smiled and suddenly she thought he looked like the man she'd met at the Savoy. 'You know, Hilary, once I was falling in love with you, although I said to myself "this woman doesn't need a man. She is the star, her own guiding light"; even so, I was going to take a chance, but then . . .' he paused, his eyes darkening making him an old man again, 'then I met Cleo. She was all the things I'd missed, all the fun, the youth . . .'

She let go of his hands and moved her chair closer to his. He put one hand out to her and they sat, hand-in-hand, looking out over the garden.

'Will it mean hospital?'

'No. I shall stay here till the end. It's such a paradise and I wanted so much to live in it and see the seasons come and go. I pray to God, just a few more months, please, let me see the bulbs flower next spring, but you can't make bargains with God, Hilary. All these wonders we take for granted, the smell of wood smoke from the bonfire, the amazing scent of roses, newly mown grass, when time begins to run out we notice these things vividly for the first time, things we took for granted . . . time, such a little word, so stark and terrible.' He was silent a moment, then he said, 'Do you pray, Hilary?'

A single tear rolled down her cheek. 'Not

consciously.'

'I think we all pray in our own way.'

'Yes,' she said, 'I think we do.'

They sat on, locked in their separate thoughts. In the distance the gardener whistled tunelessly as he tossed weeds into a wheelbarrow, pausing now and then to mop his brow with his bare arm. The water sparkled in the dancing sunlight, bird sounds erupted from the tall trees, strange single notes like sporadic bursts from a heavenly choir, moorhens rustled and twittered in the creek—summer noises on a summer's day.

'So much beauty,' said Luke, 'I wonder who will live here when I'm gone.'

CHAPTER SEVENTEEN

'Two down, one to go.' Lana's eyes were bleak. 'She just needs Rory now to make the hat trick.'

'I tried to warn Maxine so many times,' said Hilary, 'I warned her that when Alan Maxwell was ready, he might look elsewhere.' Bitterly she added, 'I didn't expect it to be Cleo.'

'Cleo is a cow,' said Lana, 'always has been and I, for one, have finished with her, absolutely and entirely.'

'Luke is blaming himself for marrying her and making her unhappy,' said Hilary, 'he's making sure she has a generous allowance to keep her going in her new life.'

'Then he's a fool,' said Lana. 'Is he going to divorce her?'

A strange look came over Hilary's face.

'No,' she said. 'He won't do that.'

'So she won't be marrying Maxwell?'

'Eh?'

Hilary seemed to have suddenly become lost in thought. 'She won't be marrying Maxwell if there's to be no divorce.'

'In time maybe,' said Hilary. Time, Luke had said, so stark, so important.

'How did Maxine take it?'

'Calmly, very calmly.' Hilary thought of Luke reciting his death sentence, Maxine had shown the same calm. 'Like someone had sliced her heart in two and she was too numb to feel the pain.'

'And?'

'She's going to Paris,' Hilary said. 'She went to her room after I'd told her. She stayed up there about an hour, then she came down, still dry-eyed, and asked if the offer of work in Paris was still open and if so how soon could she go? She's leaving tomorrow. I rang André last night and Maxine will stay with him and Solange until he can find her an apartment near her work. There are two other girls in the salon about Maxine's age. I shall, of course, check that she's all right when I visit Paris.'

'Maxine will be all right,' said Lana, 'her French is excellent. She'll find the nearest charity and start knitting shawls for the poor and perhaps, in time she'll forget that bastard and the humiliation he caused her.'

'Knitting shawls for charity is not what I want for her,' said Hilary, 'I want her to swing in Paris with the other swingers. I've put André and Solange in the picture.'

'I can't see our Maxine getting off her shapely ass to go mixing it with the gay Parisians,' said Lana, 'it's not her scene.'

'It could be,' said Hilary, 'there's nothing like a broken heart to send one on a roller coaster.'

'You're quite a philosopher, Mother.' Lana paused, then she added, 'Have you realised that Cleo will be living near you now? Can you see our Cleo in her apron trotting down to Clarrie to borrow a cup of sugar? Christ! Someone should spare some pity for that poor, stupid bastard.' She threw back her head and laughed. 'Pity him,' she said, 'he's got Cleo.' She sobered then. 'I'm sorry for Patsy, though, she's a sweet little kid. Imagine calling Cleo "Mother".'

But Hilary made no comment. She seemed to have gone far away again. Lana had noticed lately how her mother's eyes would grow suddenly sombre and her attention would wander, almost as if she had something on her mind, something, Lana thought, that had nothing to do with Cleo.

*   *   *

Molly Waring faced her nephew in the sun parlour. Outside on the lawn Patsy was pedalling her toy car.

'I shall leave immediately. If I take one case, you can send on the others.'

'But Moll,' he pleaded desperately, 'don't go yet, please. Give Cleo a chance to settle in, show her the ropes, she's not been used to house-keeping.'

'And condone your fornicating with her in Gail's bed? What do you think I am, a madam in a whorehouse?'

'You can't say that, Moll. I truly love Cleo. She loves *me*. We couldn't help falling in love. It just happened.'

Molly Waring snorted.

'Just happened! Don't give me that rubbish. I suppose Luke Madden should be grateful you didn't attend the wedding or he might not have had a honeymoon. Oh God, Alan, you disgust me! To think that I brought you up to act like this. How could you do this to Maxine who's been so good to you?'

'What's Maxine got to do with it?'

'What's Maxine got to do with it,' she repeated with a rough, incredulous laugh, 'Alan, are you blind as well as depraved?'

His voice was sullen. 'I thought that, once the flap's died down, Maxine would help Cleo with Patsy. Maxine's crazy about Patsy.'

Molly exploded then. 'Sweet Jesus Christ!' she shouted, 'Did you really imagine that Maxine would come round here as nursemaid to Patsy whilst you're fornicating with her sister?'

'I object to that word,' he said angrily, 'it's not fornication.'

A sneer twisted Molly's lips. 'Adultery then. Is that any better?'

'Cleo is my love.'

'Cleo is another man's wife.'

'Christ!' Alan shouted, 'Anyone would think we were the first two people to be in this situation. It happens every day. You want to come out of that museum, Moll.'

'Too right I do,' said Molly, 'I'm leaving right now.'

'But you can't.' He looked at his watch, 'I'm on duty. I leave for the airport in another hour. What about Patsy?'

'Fetch your fancy woman in,' snapped Molly, 'let her handle it.'

'But I shall be away till Saturday and Patsy doesn't know Cleo.'

'Too bad you didn't think of that when you were consummating your great love,' said Molly, 'but I'm sure love will find a way. The song says it does.' She walked to the stairs, his agitated voice calling to her, 'Molly, don't go, *please*.'

At the foot of the stairs she turned and flung him a wintry smile.

'Too late. I've already gone.' She paused, then she added maliciously, 'Like Maxine. *She* left for France this afternoon. Too bad you weren't on the Paris run, or you could've said goodbye to her.'

Alan's first reaction was hopeless despair. Then he realised he had to do something fast. He went to the 'phone and dialled. 'Mrs Madden's room please.' Silently he prayed, 'let Cleo be there.' He waited, then, with relief in his voice, he said. 'Oh darling, thank God you're in. Listen, darling, you must get over here at once, this very minute, just bring your night clothes, you can go back tomorrow to pack the rest.' She started to protest, but he cut her short. 'Darling, that must wait. This is urgent. This is now. You must come here at once. I'll explain later. Oh Christ, Cleo, I've got to be at the airport in an hour and there'll be no one with Patsy. I should be leaving now. Don't argue, sweet, just come.'

As he replaced the 'phone, sweat dripped from his face on to his uniform shirt collar. He felt hot, dirty and degraded. He'd never, even at the peak of Gail's illness, ever taken an aircraft out looking and feeling as he did now. As he moved away from the telephone table he looked out of the french windows at Patsy happily pedalling her car, with the doll Maxine had given her in the passenger seat by her side. Molly was going. Maxine had gone, Maxine who was always there when she was needed.

How could she have done this to him and Patsy? Fear for his daughter seized him for the first time. Reality had hit with a sickening thud. Reality, he realised wretchedly, had nothing to do with love.

CHAPTER EIGHTEEN

For the first month Alan and Cleo lived on a cloud. She had him utterly bewitched. She was like no other woman he'd ever known. Her lightning changes of mood amazed and delighted him and, luxuriating in his euphoria of sex, he failed to notice the effect on his child. Patsy was unable to cope with the inconstancy of this female who had whirled into her life and she cried every night for 'Ah Moll' and 'Masseeen'.

'Aunt Molly and Maxine have gone, pet,' Alan told her gently, 'and Cleo is your mama now.'

Alan quickly let Cleo know that he didn't like the Jameson twins so Cleo, with her usual disregard of others' feelings, dropped them. She was now sexually satisfied by her handsome lover so she stopped taking drugs, too.

She knew this thing with Alan Maxwell wouldn't last, it was riding too high, but it didn't worry her. Life was going just the way she'd planned it. Soon she would be ready for Rory. Rory wouldn't have wanted to shack up with a callow girl, but a woman of experience with scalps on her belt would be the kind of challenge he liked. Together the sky would be the limit and that would last. It had to. It was her night and day dream. So Cleo dreamed and waited and when Alan talked of their future together, she listened and made the right answers. Meantime the household quickly became a mess. Alan was unable to cope with ironing his own shirts and Cleo couldn't cook. They found the answer in the shape of a daily woman who came in five days a week from nine until five. They dined out a lot but at home they mostly lived on casseroles prepared by the 'daily', and take-aways.

Once when Patsy strayed into their bedroom and touched Cleo's teddy-bear, Cleo slapped her hard. 'Leave him alone. He's mine. He doesn't like children.' Patsy never went near the bedroom again.

Sometimes when Cleo was in what she called her riding high mood, she would take the silent child out in her Firebird and buy her fancy clothes. Her bank account was very healthy, a week after she left Luke he had paid into it a further thousand pounds. When Alan laughingly protested at Patsy's outlandish wardrobe, Cleo would hug the little girl and say 'She's going to grow up trendy like her new mama.'

Patsy never responded to these overtures. She seldom smiled now, withdrawing more and more into herself, but her father was too besotted with his new love to notice. Gail had never been a madly passionate girl and life with Cleo was like having a practised courtesan in his bed every night. Sometimes, in the dark recesses of his mind, there would be a niggling fear that he might be on a crazy downhill run that could crash at the first bend, but he quickly pushed such thoughts away. Soon Luke would divorce Cleo and, once they were married, she would settle down to housewifery.

They had been together five weeks when they had their first row. For two days Cleo had been listless and depressed, mooching round the house with her teddy-bear clutched to her chest. The 'daily' had taken to keeping Patsy with *her* whilst Alan was at work.

Alan was getting ready to go to the airport when Cleo drifted into the bedroom.

'Don't go to work today. It's a lovely day, let's go down to Cookham and go on the river, then have lunch at the Bel & Dragon.'

'Don't be silly, darling. I'm taking the Berlin flight out this morning.'

'Ring and say you're sick.'

'You know I can't do that.'

'You don't care about *me*.'

'You know I care. Look, darling, why don't you take Patsy into the park and feed the ducks?'

She flung the teddy-bear down on the bed.

'Christ! What do you think I am, a bloody nursemaid?'

Shocked, he said quietly, 'No. I thought you loved me and my child.'

Like lightning her mood changed. 'I do love you, Alan. Come to bed and I'll show you.'

Hurt still in his eyes, he said, 'Bed isn't the answer to all problems, Cleo.'

He pulled her to him and kissed her long and hard on the lips. As he released her he sighed. 'What have you done to me, my lovely witch?'

With a pout she said, 'If I had an aeroplane instead of a broomstick I'd have more power over you.'

Laughing now, he said, 'If you had any more power over me I'd be too weak to fly an aeroplane.' Then, suddenly serious, he said, 'If you've nothing planned for today, why don't you pack up your furs and jewellery and arrange for them to be returned to Luke? You might also write and ask him what he's doing about the divorce. It's five weeks now and we've heard nothing.'

'He refused to take my things back,' said Cleo, 'I asked him.'

Alan paused in the act of slipping into his jacket. 'You asked him? How? When?'

'I rang him to thank him for putting more money into my account.'

Fury consumed him. He grabbed her arms and shook her.

'You're still taking his money? What does that make me? A bloody gigolo?'

She whirled away from him, eyes blazing.

'I bought clothes for Patsy out of it. I stocked up our liquor. Where did you think the money was coming from?'

His anger died. He passed a hand wearily over his mouth. 'I didn't think . . .'

He had given Cleo the same sum each week that he'd given his aunt for housekeeping. Practicalities hadn't yet intruded into their passionate relationship, reality was drawing closer.

'I have to go now,' he said, 'or I'll be late. We'll talk when I get home.' Grimly he added, 'and, once and for all, we'll sort out the matter of your bloody ex-husband.'

'He's not my ex yet,' she said sweetly.

Alan drove to the airport in a black rage, something that had never happened when he was married to Gail. Gail, since he'd met Cleo memories of Gail had faded into oblivion.

Left to herself Cleo was miserable and lonely. She longed to talk to someone from her old life. Her mother's house was only a road away but she knew that if she called Clarrie would shut the door in her face; Clarrie had never liked her. Mother and Lana had each hung up on her when she tried to talk to them on the, 'phone. Mother, of course, was still sore at having Luke Madden whipped from under her nose just as she'd thought she'd landed him. And Lana, she would be madder still when she lost Rory as lose him she would to little sister. Cleo's thoughts turned to her third victim, Maxine, who'd flown away like a bird with her humiliation. Silly cow, why couldn't she have stayed? She was supposed to be so attached to the child. She could have stayed and still been near her beloved Alan. Cleo smiled at the thought of Maxine's torture at seeing Alan making love to her sister. Then her smile turned to anger. Damn Maxine living it up in Paris while *she* was stuck here in bloody suburbia with another woman's brat and no one to care.

She picked the teddy-bear up from the bed and, carrying him under one arm, she went to the 'phone and dialled Bunny.

CHAPTER NINETEEN

It was agreed that Maxine should have a week in Paris to get her bearings before starting work at her mother's salon. She did not, in fact, have to stay with her mother's manager—André Dupont and his wife—Solange—because, the day after Hilary first 'phoned him, André found the ideal apartment for Maxine. Hilary had told him she wanted something gracious, but preferably not a modern chrome-fitted flat. All Maxine's living expenses would be paid from London. André found the large house in an avenue of tall trees. There was a spacious hall and a minstrel gallery. Two apartments were on the ground floor, one each side of the hall, and likewise two apartments on the next floor up. Maxine's was an upstairs apartment to the left of the stairs. The two top apartments had the advantage of separate flights of steps leading up to the kitchen. The *concierge* explained that if Maxine wanted to get to the shops in a hurry, the main front door would be quicker. The *concierge* and his wife lived in one of the ground floor apartments and the other was occupied by a well-known free-lance photographer. The tenant of the other apartment on Maxine's landing was a French opera singer, who, with her companion, was currently on tour in America.

During her first week André took Maxine to the showroom and introduced her to the manager, Leon Deurille, and the two girls, Yvonne and Monique, with whom she would be working. Both girls welcomed her warmly. Monique said. 'Ah now that you are come, we shall be able to have our one and a half days' leave each week that madam promised us,' and Yvonne said. 'How nice that you speak the good English, it will be good for our English and American customers!'

Also during that week André and Solange took Maxine to lunch to meet people and one evening they gave a cocktail party in her honour. When it was over Solange said to her husband, 'That girl has surrounded herself with a belt of insulation, nothing can hurt her now. She's like a lovely doll programmed to say and do the right things and nothing more. If only someone could infuse some life into her, she'd be sensational.'

'Ah, but she *did* show some emotion,' said André, 'when she saw that lovely large kitchen in her apartment her eyes lit up, then almost at once they were sad again.'

'In Paris there are better things than kitchens to light up a girl's eyes,' replied Madame tartly.

Maxine had been in her apartment three weeks and had spoken to no one except the *concierge* and his wife. On her way up the main stairs she had seen beautiful young girls and handsome men going into the photographer's apartment, obviously models. Two or three times she had seen the photographer himself from her window as he strode down the avenue, limping ever so slightly, cameras slung over his shoulder. Once as she watched he had been standing below her window talking to two girls and she had noticed the jet blackness of his hair and the Gallic sallowness of his skin. Her window was open and she heard him speaking in rapid French, 'All cats are grey in the dark, even my Jupiter,' and one of the girls answered him in that throaty voice so typical of Frenchwomen, 'Ah, my friend, but you need a real cat to keep you warm.'

Maxine was enjoying her work and she got a great deal of pleasure in shopping for food in the markets. The old hurt flared when she saw small girls in the streets and she prayed that Cleo would be kind to Patsy.

She had just returned from posting a letter and was at the top of the wide staircase when she heard a noise below. She stopped, holding on to the rail of the minstrel gallery, and looked down. The noise had been the big front door being kicked shut. A man was staggering up to the door of the photographer's apartment, a high pile of assorted parcels clutched to his chest. He moved one hand from the pile of parcels, obviously to reach in the pocket of his jeans for the key and, as he did so, the top parcels slithered to the floor. He bent to try to retrieve them, but more cascaded down. With a muttered oath he tried to retain the few remaining but lost his balance and collapsed in a heap on the floor, parcels all round him. It was then that Maxine laughed. Starting with a giggle, gurgling laughter echoed round the now silent hall. It stopped as suddenly as it had started and Maxine clapped a hand to her mouth in consternation. Vivid blue eyes blazed up at her, the blue strangely at odds with the jet black hair and sallow complexion, and a voice speaking English with a decided Irish accent said, 'Since you find it so funny, Maxine, how about coming down and giving me a hand?'

She stared down at him in sheer amazement, eyes wide, lips parted. Maxine, he'd called her Maxine. He was scrambling up now. 'Like now, Maxine,' he called impatiently, 'stir your stumps, girl, be neighbourly, damn it.'

In a daze she slowly descended the stairs, wondering at herself for obeying the peremptory instructions of a stranger, but a stranger who knew her name.

He handed her a key and three small parcels. 'Take these and unlock the door. I'll manage the rest.'

She stood staring at him. 'You're not French.'

He grinned at her. 'No. You are. Maxine French meet Paul O'Rourke. Now lead on, Maxine, there's a good girl. I'm gasping for a drink. Make for the kitchen. It's on the right.' He gave her a gentle shove and, like Alice in Wonderland, she turned the key in the lock. She stepped into the apartment and he kicked the door shut. She stopped staring at the door on the right as if she'd seen a ghost, for there on the door panel was a poster-sized photograph of herself headed, 'Maxine—Windswept.' It showed her pausing at the foot of the front steps, both arms round a bag of groceries, her mouth twisted as she blew strands of hair from her eyes. She turned on him and demanded, 'When did you take this and how do you know my name?'

'Question one, from my window one windy day, question two, I'm MI5. Now get in, there's a good girl, these packages are heavy.'

It was like a crazy dream. What was she doing here obeying a stranger?

'Come on, Maxine,' he was urging, 'open the door.'

His sheer effrontery mesmerised her. She opened the door and got another shock for there, staring at her with hostile eyes from his perch on the wide window seat was the largest Burmese cat she'd ever seen.

'Don't be scared of Jupiter,' said the man, 'when he looks like that he's showing off. He's quite harmless really,' but Maxine was staring about her in further bewilderment. On the kitchen walls were two more poster-sized pictures of herself, one taken when she was in the park watching children play.

That was headed, 'Maxine—sad.' The other showed her walking down the avenue—that was headed, 'Maxine—Pensive.'

'Good, aren't they?' he said, dumping his parcels on the table. 'Two magazine editors have been after me to get you signed up.'

She came to life then. Her eyes blazed at him.

'You've taken a diabolical liberty and you can tell your magazine friends to go and . . .'

He stood grinning at her. 'I must get a picture of you like that. I shall call it, 'Maxine—Mad,' and now finish saying what you want me to tell my magazine buddies to do.'

'You had no right to take my picture without my permission.'

'Oh come on, Maxine, a cat may look at a king, same applies to ambitious photographers and lovely girls. Oh, I knew you weren't the sort to consider posing for a magazine, so no one's going to worry you, but model or not, we'll have to do something about re-styling your hair. It's bloody awful. We'll get Jules le Clerc to do it. Now put those parcels down and get the white plonk out of the fridge while I get the glasses.'

'Are you crazy?' she demanded. She plonked the parcels she'd been holding down on the table and marched to the door.

'Maxine,' the tone had changed. It was pleading now.

Despising herself for her weakness she paused and turned.

'Maxine, would it hurt you so much to take wine with your neighbour? I can assure you I have absolutely no designs on that fair body of yours.'

With a spirit that shocked her even as she spoke, she asked, 'Why? Are you a queer?'

He gave a great shout of laughter and then the blue eyes grew dark.

'No,' he said soberly, 'I'm not a queer, but I'm as neutered as poor bloody Jupiter over there.'

At the sound of his name the cat bounded off the window seat and rubbed himself round

Maxine's legs and, as she bent to stroke him, she knew she would stay.

After their second glass of wine he said, 'Shall we eat out or shall I rustle us up an omelette here?'

And Maxine said, 'I'll rustle up the omelettes, that is if I'm sober enough.'

She felt a strange comfort in this oddly furnished, cluttered kitchen, so unlike her immaculate kitchen upstairs. It was relaxing, too, to be able to speak English again.

Paul produced a very fine brandy after they had finished their excellent mushroom omelettes and Maxine sat on the window seat, Jupiter on her lap. As she sipped her brandy she asked sleepily, 'Why does part of you look French?'

'Because my mother is French. My father was Irish.'

'Was?'

'He's dead.'

'I'm sorry.' She gave a great sigh. 'Life is very very sad.'

'Maxine,' he said, 'you're much too pretty to go around looking like a wet week just because some silly sod's stood you up.'

Maxine tried to be indignant, but she was very drowsy. 'Look who's talking. You're in the same boat, aren't you? You should know how it feels.'

'I'm what?'

'You said you were as . . .' she paused,

'neutered as Jupiter. That means some girl's spoiled you for anyone else.'

He gave a mirthless laugh. 'No one else in Paris knows this, Maxine, but I *am* well and truly neutered. There was a girl once, we were going to marry, but I got over her long ago, just after the accident in fact.'

Maxine was wide awake now. 'What accident?'

'We lived in Northern Ireland. My father was a scientist. A friend of his was taken sick so father stood in for him to give a lecture. I went with him. On our way from the car to the college we were shot by terrorists. My father died instantly. I was lucky. Bullets went into my thigh, some embedded in the pelvic bone. The urethra was damaged, also some small perineum nerves which means I have absolutely no sensation left in my genital parts.' He gave a short laugh. 'The joke was on them, though, they killed the wrong man. The man they were gunning for was my father's friend. After the funeral we sold up, my mother came back to Nice where she lives now amongst her own family. I came to Paris and here I am, half frog, half leprechaun, a diabolical mixture. What a ram I might have been if I'd been whole.'

Hands clasped behind his head, he lay back on the ornate settee so out of place in a kitchen, and stared in rapt contemplation at the ceiling.

'And, for many a time I have been half in love with easeful death, call'd him soft names in many a mused-rhyme. That's Keats, Maxine. Morbid bugger, wasn't he?'

But Maxine was quietly weeping. She had laughed and cried today for the first time since Alan and Cleo.

CHAPTER TWENTY

Drained and exhausted, Alan got home just after midnight expecting Cleo to rush into his arms and declare her thankfulness that he was safe, but when he opened the sitting room door he found her lying on the settee, a glazed, far-away look in her eyes. He sniffed—there was a strange aroma in the room. It could have been her French cigarettes but, heavy-hearted, he knew it was not.

'The airport 'phoned you?'

'Eh?' She looked at him vaguely. She hadn't even greeted him.

'To tell you I'd be late.'

'I think so.'

'Don't you know?'

'I forget. I've been busy.'

'It was a pretty hairy ride. First time in my flying career that an engine's died on me.'

Now that it was over and his crew and passengers were safe, he wanted to talk to someone about it, to get it out of his system, but Cleo was smiling into space. The thought came to him that Gail and Maxine would have cared. Suddenly desperately lonely he asked her, 'Cleo, what have you been smoking?'

She turned on him a sweet, angelic smile. 'Just a teeny joint. Polly was here. I was bored, so bored, I asked her to come. She left me some. Have one, Alan, then you'll feel better.'

'In *my* job? Are you crazy?' He hauled her to her feet and she staggered when he let go of her. 'Now listen, Cleo, I will not have this kind of thing in my house with Patsy. Besides, we could be busted. I could lose my job.'

She gave a little giggle. 'Then lose it. I'll give you some money. Tonight I was celebrating.'

Sick at heart he asked, 'Celebrating what?'

'Luke,' she said. She clasped her hands together like an excited child. 'Luke has shot himself,' she said. 'If he hasn't changed his will, I'll be rich.'

* * *

'He planned it down to the last detail,' Hilary said, 'this is the letter he left me.'

Lana took the letter and leaned back in the armchair in her mother's office.

'You look tired,' Hilary said.

'I am. I was up all night.'

Lana's eyes narrowed as she started to read aloud. 'I think the end is very near. I'm too much of a coward to wait for it.' She looked up from the letter. 'What did he mean?'

'He had a brain tumour,' said Hilary. 'It was incurable.'

'Oh, my God!' After a pause whilst she digested this shocking information Lana went on reading. 'I so much appreciate our quiet dinners together, Hilary, you have meant so much to me in my last days. I shall go out thinking of you. My lawyer will see to the sale of my lovely Honiton Hall and compensate the staff until they can get fresh employment, but I want you, Hilary, to have the final say in getting the right purchaser for my home. I leave all my pictures to you. I know you like them because you helped me choose them. The rest, of course, is Cleo's.'

Lana put the letter back on the desk.

'So Cleo will marry Alan Maxwell now and spend like there's no tomorrow.'

'I wouldn't bet on her marrying him,' said Hilary, 'things aren't all honey in the Maxwell love nest. Their "daily" gossips about them to Clarrie in the Parade post office. She apparently hates Cleo and is sorry for him and the child.'

'Serves him right,' said Lana, 'but I'm sorry for little Patsy, poor mite.'

Hilary looked at her daughter, realising suddenly that it was only half-past nine and Lana had walked in just after nine.

'What brings you to Town so early, Lana?'

'I stayed in Bankside General all night,' said Lana, 'Rory was knifed last evening as he left his office. They took him in there.'

'Oh my God!' said Hilary, starting up, 'is he . . .?'

'Out of danger now. At first they didn't know. That's why I stayed.'

'Who did it?'

Lana gave a wintry smile. 'There were no witnesses. Just someone didn't like the colour of his eyes. This note was handed in at the hospital for me. Fortunately the police had left by then.'

Puzzled and disturbed, Hilary unfolded the sheet of paper Lana had taken from a grubby envelope. Crudely printed were the words—'If lover-boy survives this, ask him if he's so keen to mess with Susie now.'

Hilary raised shocked eyes to her daughter. 'Susie? His first wife?'

Lana nodded, taking back the note which she carefully folded before putting it back into the envelope.

'God! I'm bushed,' she said.

'Is Rory still involved with his first wife, Lana?'

Lana yawned. 'Seems like it, doesn't it? Silly old me, I trusted the bastard.'

'Aren't you going to take the note to the police?'

'No. I'm not going to let him think it's that important. Besides, dirty linen laundering is not my scene.'

'I think the police should see the note. Rory might have been killed.'

Lana gave a tired smile. 'Then it would have been even less important.'

She pulled herself upright. 'I have one call to make, then I shall go home to sleep.' She stood up. 'I'm so terribly sorry about Luke. He was a nice man.'

'Contact with our family didn't do him much good,' said Hilary.

'Oh, I don't know,' said Lana, 'he had *you*.'

Hilary looked up sharply, suspecting sarcasm, but Lana's smile was kind.

'I'll ring you this evening, Mother,' she said. Then she was gone.

CHAPTER TWENTY ONE

'We got no fancy trappings, Mrs Jefferson,' said Joe Wallis, 'except for them two armchairs. Rory don't believe in all them plush trimmings.'

Lana glanced round her husband's office. 'I can see that. It's hardly Ewing Oil, is it?'

Joe grinned weakly. 'We got booze. You like a drink, Mrs Jefferson?'

'No, thanks,' said Lana, 'and, for God's sake, stop calling me Mrs Jefferson. My name's Lana and well you know it.'

Joe uttered a little nervous laugh. 'Yeh, well,

Mrs . . . Lana. I'm sure glad Rory's gonna be OK. I bin worried outer me skull. You musta bin, too. What can I do fer you, Mrs . . . Lana?'

Lana thrust the grubby envelope into his hand. 'Give him this when you see him. I received it while I was in the hospital last night. Apparently a small boy said a man paid him to deliver it. Go on, you can read it.'

Joe's eyes hardened as he read the note.

'Them bleedin' Potters.' He raised anxious eyes to Lana. 'Rory's never done nothin' wrong with Susie. You gotta believe it, Lana.' A note of caution crept into his voice. 'The coppers en't seen this?'

'No,' said Lana. 'They'd gone before it was handed in.'

'That's a relief. It wouldn't do no good fer the Old Bill to see this.' Joe shook his head. 'The silly sod should've told you hisself. What happened was, and this is gospel, Susie's sister rang here, said Suse was in the sh . . . in a mess and might do 'erself in. Rory went round and paid 'er rent. Some neighbours told Potter and he beat her up. Rory went ter see the poor little perisher in 'ospital, a right mess she was *and* she lost the kid she was expectin' too. Then Rory went ter see Potter.'

'And found him?'

A smile of pure joy lit Joe's face. 'Oh yes,' he said softly, 'he found him. Potter couldn't walk proper fer a week.'

'And now Potter's fixed Rory?'

'Not Ron,' said Joe, 'his ol' man and one of 'is brothers I bet, *and* I bet they got cast-iron alibis. Ron Potter's in Huddersfield, so they can't pin it on 'im.' Joe paused, grinning, 'Like they won't be able ter pin it on me when the Potters gets theirs. Not that the coppers gonna wear their boots out to find who fitted up the Potters, hand out a bonus more like.'

Lana looked at him steadily. 'Must you, Joe?'

His grin died. 'Yeh,' he said, 'I must.'

'But then there'll be no end to it.'

'Yes there will,' said Joe, 'because when they're in 'ospital gettin' over their mugging by person or persons unknown, I shall call with a bunch of flowers and what I shall tell them will ensure Rory's safety fer the rest of 'is natural.'

'I see,' said Lana. 'As we say in the underworld, you got something on them.'

'Too right,' said Joe with a quiet laugh. 'I got something on them all right.'

'You're very loyal, Joe.'

'He's a good mate ter me is Rory. Always knew he'd get on. There was this time when we was kids and old man Garney was chuckin' old flower-pots inter 'is dustbin. Rory goes up ter 'im, all perlite, and asks if he could 'ave 'em. Garney said 'yes' and we fetched our kid's pram an' loaded them. Then we took 'em to a nursery three miles out of town and flogged 'em. That was Rory's first deal. The only mistake he made after that was marryin' Suse.

She was never in ’is class.’

‘Where is Susie now?’

‘Rory heard she was workin’ in a pub near Slough what belongs to ’er Aunt Jess, the Flag and Bugle.’

‘I want to see her.’

Joe was startled. ‘No, Mrs Jefferson, I mean Lana, no, Rory wouldn’t like that.’

‘Bugger Rory,’ said Lana, ‘the Flag and Bugle near Slough.’ She stood up. ‘You needn’t look so scared, Joe, I’m not going to hit her or bawl her out. I just want to see her. We have a lot in common, we’re both stooges for the same comedian.’

‘Suse en’t your type, Lana,’ said Joe, ‘and Rory wouldn’t never take you in or do anything ter hurt you. That I know fer sure.’

Lana smiled. ‘I’m sure he deserves such blind loyalty.’

She walked to the door. ‘Thanks for the chat, Joe. If I were not so tired I’d ask you to give me a drink, but if I have one now I shall fall asleep driving home.’

Walking beside her Joe said, ‘They said ’e was sleepin’ when I rang. Thought I’d go in ternight, but if you’re gonna be there . . .’

‘I shan’t be,’ said Lana. ‘I stayed at the hospital all last night. I shall catch up on some sleep now.’ She patted his arm. ‘Don’t forget to show him the note and then destroy it.’

‘It might upset him.’

‘So?’

'So he might have a relapse.'

'Joe,' she said softly, 'don't be such a bloody old woman. It spoils your image.'

He grinned feebly. 'I take it you don't want me to tell him then that you believe there's nothin' goin' on between him and Suse?'

'You take it right,' said Lana, 'let the bugger sweat for a bit, like he's made *me* do.'

Joe's grin this time held sheer adoration.

* * *

As Lana pushed open the door of the saloon bar of the Flag and Bugle, the smell of beer and hot cooking oil assailed her nostrils. Men and a few women sat at tables eating off large plates piled high with oven-cooked chips. Fishy and meaty smells hung on the steamy air. A red-headed woman stood behind the bar polishing a glass tankard. Her naturally aggressive face hardened as Lana approached, acknowledging that this was not the Flag and Bugle's usual type of customer. At the woman's side stood a slight, sandy-haired man of about thirty who paused in the act of pulling a pint to gawp at Lana in open admiration.

'Yes?' snapped the woman.

'Is Susie Potter here?'

The woman's eyes narrowed with suspicion. 'Who wants 'er?'

'Lana Jefferson.' As the woman opened her mouth to speak, Lana held up her right hand. 'I come in peace.'

The man grinned. 'Pale face want pow-wow with squaw? No need to call in the cavalry, Jess.' He turned and yelled through an open door at the back of the bar, 'Someone ter see yer, Suse.'

'Thanks, chief,' Lana said and they exchanged grins while the woman assessed Lana with hostile eyes. When the girl came slowly into the bar Lana thought she looked like a child dressed up in play. Enormous swinging cherries dragged at her ears and a comb with matching cherries was stuck into a wispy top-knot of hair. She had a sweet, vacant face and Lana thought Rory must have been very young when he took this one on, rather like a small boy with a pet kitten. She held out her hand.

'I'm Lana Jefferson.'

The pale blue eyes widened with shock, but the girl let her hand lay limply in Lana's grasp. Lana gave her a friendly smile. 'Could we have a little chat, Susie?'

Before Susie could reply the man lifted the bar flap to let Lana through and ushered her and Susie into the back room. The woman called after them. 'Don't be long, Suse, we're gettin' busy an' if you need help, call.'

Inside the fusty parlour the two women faced each other.

'I promise you won't have to call, Susie,' said Lana, 'I'm not armed. I came because I wanted to tell you in case you've heard some garbled version, Rory's been knifed, he's in hospital but . . .'

Susie put a hand to her throat, with the other hand she reached for a chair-back.

'He's OK,' Lana said. 'He's out of danger.'

Susie sank down in the chair. 'Them Potters,' she said bitterly, 'I knew they'd do it when Rory done Ron and it's all my fault.'

'No it's not,' said Lana, 'it's the stupid mug's own fault. Anyway, the score is even now. Joe Wallis has promised me that it's at an end.'

'Joe,' the girl murmured. 'He's a good scout.' She raised her eyes to Lana. 'It was good of you to come. It en't exactly your kind of dive, is it?'

'Oh I don't know,' said Lana, 'it could have been. My mother once worked in an East End sweatshop, you know. Anyway, the other reason I came here, Susie, was to say that if you're ever in trouble again like you were when Rory helped you with your rent, I want you to come to me, not him. You'll find you'll get a lot more sense and practical help from me.' She took a card from her bag and gave it to Susie who had risen from the chair to lean against the table. 'I mean it, Susie, any time. I'll always be pleased to hear from you, even if it's only that you need to talk or want advice.'

The girl's eyes filled with tears.

'Hey, don't cry,' said Lana, 'there's nothing to cry about.'

'Yes there is,' Susie gulped, 'See, I never

thought of you bein' like this. I had you down for some toffee-nosed bitch. I can see now why he fell fer yer. Against you I never had a chance. I'll always love 'im, y'know. I can't help it.'

'I know,' said Lana gently, 'it happens like that sometimes.'

'When he come ter see me 'bout my rent, I arst him to make love ter me.'

Lana tensed ever so slightly but, with a tiny smile, the girl went on, 'Went all moral on me, 'e did. 'E must think an awful lot of *you*.' She looked at Lana steadily through her tears. 'You do reely love 'im, don't you?'

'Yes,' said Lana, 'I do really love him.'

'That's OK then.' Susie took a tissue from her sleeve and dabbed at her eyes. 'Good men is hard to find. Sandy, the bloke what works in the bar here, he's ever so good ter me. He says when I get free of Ron, me and him orter get together.'

'And would you like that?'

Susie smiled wanly. 'Could do worse, I s'pose. When you see Rory, will you give 'im my love and tell 'im I'm sorry?'

'When I see him I surely will,' said Lana. She turned at the door and smiled at her husband's first wife. 'Be lucky, Susie,' she said, 'Goodbye.'

* * *

Three days later Joe stood beside the bed

looking down at his boss. Rory grimaced with pain as he rolled over to face him.

'Still 'urts, then?' asked Joe anxiously.

'Course it bleedin' hurts. What you think they did it with? A darning needle?' Then Rory smiled weakly. 'Sorry, I blow me top easy these days. Now tell me about it. What you do? Take the wheels off old man Potter's motor?'

'Nah,' said Joe, 'the way 'e is 'e won't need no motor fer a while. They was all done over real sweet, Pa Potter the worst. Cor struth, Rory, you'd 'ave wet yourself laughin' ter see me at St George's Hospital standin' by Pa Potter's bed with a bag of grapes, sour they was, too. I tried 'em in the market before I bought 'em. I was walkin' without fear, see, on account of me alibi in Bedford when the Potters was beat up. Roly and Pete did a sweet job, even so, I wish I could've done it meself. Anyhow, I says to Potter, I says, you better 'ope Rory stays 'ealthy from now on, I says, 'cos the minute 'e comes apart, a certain legal gent in the City's gonna send the Yard all the crap on that Wandsworth job where them two guards got topped. It's all there I says, witnesses' attested statements, pictures, the whole shootin' match, sorry, no pun intended I says, an' I said the only daylight you'll see then, mate, will be by courtesy of 'er Madge's narks in the shovel. As fer nookie, well the old mind boggles, but then, I says, of course you'd know all about that.'

Rory listened in silence to Joe's recital, then

he asked, 'And who exactly is this fancy City geyser got all the "gen" on the Wandsworth job then?'

Joe looked at him blankly. 'How the hell should *I* know?'

Rory laughed and winced with pain. 'And Potter believed it?'

'Oh he believed it,' said Joe. 'Remember, at the time, the police said there was witnesses and arst 'em to come forward.'

'Yeh,' said Rory. 'I remember. You've done a great job, Joe, thanks.' His eyes darkened. 'Tell me again what Lana said when she gave you that bleeding note.'

'Cor, guv,' Joe protested, 'I told you already a dozen times. Simply said, "show 'im this and then destroy it", and I arst her had the Old Bill seen it and she said, "No."'

'And you really told her it wasn't true about me and Susie?'

Joe remembered the amusement in Lana's lovely eyes when she said, 'Let the bugger sweat.' He shrugged. 'I tried to tell 'er, guv, but you know women . . .'

Rory punched his forehead hopelessly with one hand. 'She won't even come and see me. I ring but she won't talk to me, just says, "Get well soon", and hangs up, like I was a bloody stranger. Would you talk to her again, Joe, make her see sense?'

'Not me, mate, I'm no marriage guidance counsellor.'

'Damn!' said Rory. 'Damn! Damn! Damn!'

Joe grinned down at him. 'Don't worry, mate,' he said, 'with your brains and charm you'll find some way to get yer tootsies back under the table.'

CHAPTER TWENTY TWO

'I don't see why we can't get married right away,' said Alan. He spoke with little conviction. Marriage to Cleo now wasn't so attractive as it had been in the beginning, but something had to be done to stabilise their relationship which seemed to be fast falling apart.

'It wouldn't be decent,' said Cleo, 'he's only just died.'

'It's a bit late to be talking of decency, isn't it?'

Why didn't I realise at the start, Cleo asked herself, that Alan, for all his sexual prowess in bed, is just a stiff-necked bore? It's good that he'll be out of my life soon. Happiness swelled inside her. She was flying already although she'd only taken one of the pills Polly had given her. Today of all days, she told herself firmly, I must keep my feet on the ground because today is the day that will completely change my life, mine and Rory's. No one in the family will ever speak to either of us again, but who cares about that? I've got money. Rory loves money. Aloud she said, 'It's good that Luke didn't change his will.'

Alan eyed her with disgust. 'I meant what I said, Cleo. I don't intend to touch a penny of Luke Madden's money.'

'I'll settle some on you,' she said airily, 'then you can ditch your stupid old job.'

'Thanks,' he said bitterly, 'but my stupid old job is all I've got left of my self-respect and I don't intend to take money from *you*, Cleo. Let me make that quite clear.'

Cleo picked up her handbag. He stood there accusing, handsome in his uniform, flint in his eyes where once there had been adoration, but she didn't care. He was soft, not hard like Rory.

'Are you going out?'

'Yes. Dancy's promised to stay till I get back.'

'And when will that be?'

'Some time this afternoon.'

'Be sure you get back then because I've got to get off to work now and I don't want Patsy dumped on neighbours by Mrs Dancy again. Anyway, where are you going?'

'If it's of any interest to *you*,' she said loftily, 'hospital visiting.'

* * *

'She's quieter now,' Polly said to her brother. 'God, she was in a state when I found her. I've cleaned up the bathroom, she'd been sick all over the floor. It was disgusting. God knows how long she's been here. We shouldn't have given her a key, Bunny, God knows who she might bring in when she gets stoned.'

'What's her trouble today?'

Polly frowned. 'Dunno exactly, first she was sobbing quietly, then the next minute she was shrieking something about a hospital and someone calling her terrible names. "And then he laughed at me," she said, "he laughed at me and said he'd never wanted me at all, it was just a game."'

Bunny shrugged. 'Another set-to with Maxwell I suppose.'

'I don't think so,' said Polly. 'From her ravings I gathered it was some other guy, she muttered something about going to leave Alan for him. Anyway, I've got to go now. Pull her together and come over to Rita's place. She's got plenty of goods and it'll be some party.'

Bunny found Cleo on the bed. She stared at him with glassy eyes. Her lips quivered. 'I'm scared of hospitals.'

'Me too,' said Bunny, 'so no one's going to hospital.'

'He was sitting by the bed,' she said, 'in silk pyjamas. He looked wonderful.'

'Well he would in silk pyjamas, wouldn't he?' said Bunny. 'Who are we talking about by the way, comrade?'

She started to shudder and her teeth

chattered. 'I'm cold.'

'I'll warm you, baby.'

Bunny cradled her in his arms until the shaking gradually stopped, then he eased her up. 'Better now?'

'I'll never be better.'

'Yes you will. Come on now, let's fix you up, then we'll get in that red flier of yours and zoom over to Rita's. We'll soon have you floating, baby, nirvana, Cleo, peace.'

'Left Patsy, goblins.' Cleo gave a crazy laugh, 'Goblins get *me*.'

'Yeh,' said Bunny 'good old goblins, eh?' He pulled her off the bed and propelled her to the door.

'Head under the cold tap, sweetheart, then we'll hit the road.'

As she staggered towards the bathroom he did a mock war dance round her. 'You're rich, baby,' he chanted, 'you own the world.'

* * *

Lana sniffed. 'Which nurse uses Chanel?'

'Cleo was here.'

Trying to keep her voice light, Lana said, 'And what did Florence Nightingale want?'

'Me, gift-wrapped in Luke Madden's money.'

'And?'

'And nothing.'

Lana studied the picture on the wall. 'Don't

tell me you don't have the hots for her like all the others.'

'Are you out of your tiny mind? I wouldn't have the hots for Cleo if I was alone with her on a desert island and there were no other women left.'

Lana gave a faint smile. 'You and Cleo and the end of the world.'

'Forget that little tramp,' he said, unsmiling, 'Why the hell haven't you been to see me, Lana?'

'I stayed with you all night when they brought you in.'

'Big deal! Every day I waited for you.'

'You had no choice. Your get-up-and-go's a bit hampered at the moment, isn't it? Anyway, you weren't neglected, I fixed up the private room and sent in pyjamas and dressing-gown.'

'Big of you. I hope it didn't interfere too much with your social round. May I ask why I'm honoured with a visit now?'

'I came to tell you I'll be picking you up tomorrow. Sister says you can go home if you promise to rest when you get there. I hear you haven't exactly been a model patient. Why? Aren't the nurses pretty enough?'

'You said home?'

She eyed him coolly. 'Right. You got something else in mind? Moving in with little Miss Money-Bags for instance?'

'It's my body that's sick,' he said, 'not my brain. Home will do fine if you and the kids are there. Lana, please believe me, that note about Susie was rubbish.'

'Oh I know that,' she said, 'Joe told me the morning after the attack.'

'And you believed him?'

'Of course I believed him. He's a good man, is Joe.'

'Did he know you believed him?'

'Of course. Why shouldn't he?'

He picked up a magazine from the bed cover and slung it to the foot of the bed. 'The sly bastard! He let me sweat here thinking . . . Christ, Lana, if you knew it was lies, why didn't you come and see me before?'

She grinned down at him. 'Just felt like giving you a bad time.'

He grabbed her hand and pulled her down to him, wincing at the effort.

'You certainly did that, you and bloody Joe between you.'

She disengaged her hand and straightened up.

'I love you, Lana.'

'Good,' she said, 'and next time you decide to pay a dolly-bird's rent, make sure her husband doesn't find out. By the way, Susie sent her love to you and said to tell you she was sorry.'

'What?'

'Susie sent her love,' said Lana calmly, 'I went to Slough to see her. She's a nice little thing, but definitely not your type. Next time she's in trouble she's coming to *me*. We neither of us go much on this underworld stuff, little boys playing at mafiosi.'

'Christ!' exploded Rory, 'women! Devious, deceitful, sly . . .'

'But good in bed.'

'Yeh,' he said with a grin, 'bloody good in bed.'

'But not yet,' said Lana, 'not until we're much stronger.'

'*We* are strong enough now,' said Rory.

'No,' said Lana firmly, '*we* are not.'

At that moment the door opened and a nurse entered with a cup of coffee on a tray. She stopped short at the sight of Lana.

'My wife,' said Rory easily, 'she couldn't come before. She's been in quarantine with spots.'

* * *

Alan was surprised to see a light in Patsy's bedroom as he drove up the drive at 11 o'clock. Was she ill? As he started to open the garage doors he heard a movement in the shrubbery which edged the drive. Startled, he swung round and the small figure in its nightgown hurtled towards him and flung herself into his arms.

'Patsy!' He picked her up and cradled her to him. 'What on earth are you doing out here?'

The child was whimpering as she buried her

face into his neck. Leaving the car where it was, he carried the little girl indoors. The front door was wide open and there were lights in all the downstairs rooms.

'Cleo,' he shouted, 'Cleo.'

He put the child down on the settee, took off his jacket and wrapped it round her. 'What happened, Patsy?'

The child's face was dirty, bits of the shrubbery were in her hair, her cheeks were blotchy with tears and her little body heaved with spasmodic sobs.

'Goblins get Patsy.'

'There are no goblins, Patsy. You're all right now, daddy's here and he won't let anyone hurt you.' She gave another great sob and closed her eyes. Safe now, she was dropping off to sleep.

Alan closed the door and strode through the downstairs rooms. Muttering an oath he returned and picked up the child. 'Come on, darling, let's get you cleaned up a bit, then you can sleep in daddy's bed.'

The child nodded thankfully, her eyes still closed, the little body still jerking with sobs. When Alan had washed her face and hands he put her into his bed which was unmade and smelled strongly of Cleo's perfume.

'Daddy's just going to put the car away, then we'll both go to sleep.'

Patsy made no answer. She was already fast asleep. Alan was gripped in a tight fury such as he'd never experienced before. He thanked

God that it was a mild night. Even so, the child would probably take a long time to get over the shock. His fury increased as the possibilities flooded into his mind. Patsy could have been assaulted, kidnapped, the house burgled; the mind boggled. Bitch, he thought, the bolts go on the doors tonight and if you come back you can bloody well sleep in that sardine-can you call a car. He was just closing the front door when he heard a muffled explosion and saw a sheet of flame shoot skywards. He shuddered. Another accident, a bad one this time, up there on that bend in the main road where once Maxine had so skilfully averted disaster when she was driving his car—Maxine of the quiet voice and caring eyes. Dear Maxine, why did you have to go away? He heard the police and ambulance sirens in the distance as, sick at heart, he bolted the doors and went upstairs to his daughter.

CHAPTER TWENTY THREE

They came from far and wide to Cleo's funeral. The manageress of the Manchester salon talked quietly to André and Solange Dupont who had flown over from Paris that morning. The three girls from the London salon stood together awaiting the arrival of the hearse.

'I never liked her,' said one, 'but you can't

help feeling shocked at her going so young, such a terrible way to die, too.'

'Any way to die is terrible,' said the junior smoothing down the skirt of her black off-the-peg suit which she thought looked every bit as good as the model suit worn by Lana Jefferson.

'I heard she was on drugs.'

Maris Judson, head of sales, gave a little shudder. 'They say that Firebird of hers went up in the air and turned over twice before it burst into flames, just like a stunt on films. And that tanker ...' she shuddered again. 'I always hate driving past those fuel tankers, bloody tinder boxes.'

'Me too,' said another, 'poor tanker driver never had a prayer, did he? and that Jameson boy, they say he's only got a slim chance and even if he lives, he'll probably be paralysed. No one seems to know which one of 'em was driving.'

'I must say Madame's a hard one,' said Maris, 'looks like she's going to a fashion show.'

Hilary, flanked by Lana and Clarrie the housekeeper, watched impassively as the hearse rolled smoothly to a stop at the door of the chapel. My third funeral in less than a year, she thought, and this time I'm the chief mourner.

Alan Maxwell stood well away from the others with his friend, Bill Brandon, who, with his wife—Felice—had come to give him support. Alan looked in vain for Maxine, but Maxine it seemed had not come home for her sister's funeral.

Cleo's friend, Polly Jameson, was present accompanied by two girls. All three looked as if they were high on drugs. Their dry eyes were blank and their faces set in expressionless masks. The Jameson parents were not at the funeral. They were at the bedside of their son, Bunny, who had been smashed up in Cleo's car.

Lana tried not to look as the coffin was shouldered by the undertakers' men. She tried instead to think of Rory at home, still weak, but playing his military games of drilling the twins who were ecstatic at having him to themselves. She tried not to think of Cleo who had wanted Rory, but who lay there now in that gleaming box unable to break any more hearts.

As she entered the chapel on Lana's arm, Hilary thought I am an unnatural mother unable to weep for my children. She stared out of the chapel window as the service droned on, steadfastly keeping her eyes away from the coffin. In the distance she saw a garden and a child running down the path on chubby, wobbly legs and, suddenly, she saw another child, the baby Cleo, on the beach in summer time, running with her bucket to get water for Maxine's sand pool, her beloved teddy-bear tucked under one arm, she saw the dimpled legs, the cherubic baby smile. She looked away from the child in the distant garden just in time to see the curtains closing over the table whereon rested Cleo's coffin. She remembered someone outside saying, 'They put that old teddy-bear in with her.' The curtains closed. The coffin had gone. 'My baby!' choked Hilary and then the tears came, pouring down her cheeks in a flood, tears that were so many long years overdue. Lana put an arm round her, weeping now herself.

'Good Lord!' one of the salon girls whispered, 'Madame's human after all.'

Hilary's composure had returned by the time the mourners straggled out of the chapel. As she stepped outside Alan Maxwell approached her.

'Mrs French, I have to ask you . . .'

Hilary stopped and looked at him, her face expressionless.

'I have to ask you about her clothes, her jewellery. You see,' he went on miserably, 'I was hoping that maybe you would take them.'

'Sell them.' Hilary paused, then she said, 'What about the tanker driver's family? They could surely do with the money.'

'Yes,' he said, 'I had thought that, too.'

'The jewellery will be worth quite a lot,' said Hilary composedly, 'and the clothes, too. If you like, I'll write down the names and addresses of reliable dealers and my housekeeper can drop the list through your letter-box.'

'I'm very grateful,' he said, then, as Hilary started to turn away, he said, 'Mrs French, I'm

so very, very sorry.'
She nodded, smiled faintly and walked away.
As Alan rejoined his friends his eyes searched through the departing mourners in the desperate hope that she might have come at the last minute, but Maxine was not there.

* * *

Maxine pushed Jupiter's nose gently back as she inserted a small mat under the cat's bowl.
Paul chuckled. 'Poor old Jupiter! You'll have him wiping his feet next.'
'Well, he's a messy eater,' said Maxine, 'and I don't want him throwing cat food all over my kitchen floor. Yours is another matter, it's scruffy anyway.'
They sat in companionable silence watching the big cat munching away at his food. Nowadays Jupiter spent almost as much time in Maxine's apartment as he did in Paul's and Maxine, in fact, kept a store of cat-food tins in her pantry. Covertly appraising her, Paul congratulated himself on a job well done. Even a cocky bastard like me, he thought, had never envisaged her being such a hit, this lovely Maxine with her new *gamine* hair style, her new confidence.
'I'm a coward,' she said suddenly. 'I should have gone.'
'Was that why you didn't go to the funeral, because you were afraid to see him?'

'Yes.'

'You still care that much?'

'I shall always care,' she said simply. She twisted her fingers reslessly. 'I'm not ready to face up to things yet. I feel so safe here in Paris with you. We had a Wendy house once in our garden at home and if anyone was cross with me, I used to shut myself inside and pretend there was nothing difficult or unpleasant outside. I was in a sort of cocoon. That's how it is now.'

'I know,' he said, 'I've been there, but you have to come out some time, Maxie.'

Her eyes darkened with sudden apprehension. 'But you'll be here?'

'Reckon so. As our Yankee cousins would say, I don't aim to go no place, hon. I'll be around to be godfather to your quads and teach them the facts of life.'

The tension eased. Truth, comfort and loyalty blazed in those blue Irish eyes. Trust, she thought comfortably, what a lovely word.

'I often wonder why you bothered to take those pictures of me when you get such stunning girls coming to your studio. Was it because you were sorry for me?'

He gave a snort of disgust. 'Sorry for you? I should co-co. I thought you needed a great big wallop on your gorgeous little bum, a lovely young girl mooning around like bloody Niobe.'

'Who's bloody Niobe?'

'God, Maxie, you're diabolically ignorant,

aren't you?'

'Yes,' she agreed complacently, 'I was never very clever at school. The only thing I was any good at was French; oh, and needlework.'

Paul got up and stretched. 'Let's take a turn round the block and walk off that super meal. You're a stunning cook, Maxie.'

'I know,' she said smugly.

'And you're no modest violet either, are you? What are you planning to wear to Jules' disco tomorrow night?'

'The silver top and those new black pants you bullied me into buying.'

He nodded approval. 'Great, and watch out for Ferdy the Groper this time.'

She grinned at him. 'That's why I'm wearing pants.'

'That won't stop him, he has been known to . . .'

She held up her hands. 'OK. Spare me the sordid details. Oh, while you're here, I want to measure the sweater against your chest. It's not growing very fast I'm afraid. I'm out so much that there isn't a lot of time for knitting.'

As she held the half-finished front against his chest she said complacently, 'I chose well. That blue is the exact shade of your eyes. You must always wear black pants with the sweater to match your black hair.'

'What about something to match my complexion?'

Eyes glinting she said, 'There isn't a shade

called sallow.'

'I am not sallow.'

'Oh yes, you are,' she said, 'but it's quite attractive, a fascinating combination. When I first saw you . . .' she broke off with a giggle, the same giggle that had started her laughter at the top of the stairs.

'When you first saw me,' said Paul, 'I was on my arse in the hall surrounded by parcels and you laughed, heartless female that you are.'

Still laughing, Maxine said, 'I'm sorry, but you looked so funny.'

And there was such hurt in those lovely eyes when the brief laughter died, he remembered.

He took the knitting from her and put it on a chair.

'Come on, let's take that walk.'

'What about loading the dish washer?'

'You can do that when we get back.'

'*I* can? I cooked the dinner, remember.'

'All right, *we* can.'

'Know what *I* think?'

'I haven't got my crystal ball.'

'I think you only made friends with me to get your cooking done.'

'Too right. Top marks. Anyway, next week we'll eat out every night.'

'I prefer my own cooking.'

He rolled his eyes in mock agony. 'Ye gods and jumping Jupiters! Come on, Maxie, let's get walking. I need some air.'

She smiled and put her hand in his. No one

else had ever called her Maxie.

CHAPTER TWENTY FOUR

'I chose the Savoy grill,' said Hilary, 'because it was here that I first met Luke on his return to England. Must be getting sentimental in my old age.'

His eyes appraising her, Rory thought Hilary looks sensational tonight, young enough to be Lana's sister.

'I approve your choice, Mother,' said Lana, 'now what is this weighty matter we have to discuss?'

'Luke's estate,' replied Hilary, 'it's taking an awfully long time to settle, but it's now been definitely established that neither Luke or his first wife—Elsie-Jane—had any living relatives. Therefore, as Cleo's next-of-kin, everything comes to me; which will, of course, mean that you, Lana, and Maxine will share.' She looked steadily, first at Lana then at Rory. 'It's a very great deal of money—a big responsibility. As you know, I've just returned from seeing Maxine in Paris. I went to make a proposal to her. Now I'm going to make the same one to you. I won't tell you Maxine's decision until you tell me yours and I want you both to be absolutely truthful, to tell me what you really feel.'

Lana glanced at her husband. 'I think we usually do.'

'Well,' said Hilary, 'let's fortify ourselves with another round of drinks before I start.'

When more martinis had been placed before them, Hilary said, 'My proposal is to turn Honiton Hall into a home for the terminally sick elderly, something like the Sue Ryder homes, and Luke's money would be used to run it. The present staff would be retained, with additions, of course. Its designation would be "Honiton Hall founded by Luke Madden and his wife—Elsie-Jane". After all, it was *her* money in the first place that made Luke a rich man and he loved her very much.'

Lana didn't hesitate. 'I think it's a wonderful idea.'

Hilary looked at Rory. 'It's a lot of money,' she said, 'there would be endless possibilities for you, Rory, think well before you let Lana cast it aside.'

'I don't need to,' he said, 'I, too, think it's a great idea.'

'He's already had Luke's money offered to him once,' said Lana softly.

'Any money I have,' Rory said, 'I prefer to earn myself.'

Looking at him now, Hilary thought that since his knifing and Cleo's death Rory had lost some of his jauntiness. She decided that the new, more serious image suited him and when grey started to edge his hair he would be devastating.

'Well, that's our decision, Mother,' said Lana. 'What was Maxine's?'

'Can't you guess?' asked Hilary, coming out of her contemplation of her son-in-law. 'The same as yours of course.'

'Then that's settled,' said Lana. 'Let us know if we can help. Now, how was Maxine and what's she doing with herself?'

'She's well,' said Hilary, 'and she's knitting.'

'There you go,' declared Lana triumphantly, 'What did I tell you? Living dangerously, that's our Maxine.'

'Our Maxine,' said Hilary, 'is knitting a bright blue sweater for a very dynamic young man who has the apartment below hers.'

Lana's eyes widened in surprise. 'No!'

Rory grinned. 'These Frenchmen!'

'He's half French, half Irish,' said Hilary, 'he's a freelance photographer. He has a large cat called Jupiter who spends a great deal of time in Maxine's apartment and an old Citröen car which Maxine drives and which he calls Jezebel.'

'Struth!' said Rory, 'that doesn't sound like Maxine's scene.'

'He has large pictures of her all over his apartment,' said Hilary, 'and he tells me she's had several offers of modelling work. There's one lovely picture—a close-up of Maxine and the cat—and he's going to send me copies. I'll let you have one.'

'I can't believe it,' said Lana. 'Our Maxine. Are they in love then?'

Hilary looked thoughtful as she sipped her drink.

'It's the oddest thing,' she said slowly, 'I'm sure they love each other, but I'm equally sure they're not in love. It's really the most peculiar relationship, Maxine seems to have lots of admirers and Paul teases her about them, almost like a brother would.'

'Well,' said Lana doubtfully, 'I just hope she won't get hurt again.'

'Paul won't hurt her,' said Hilary positively, 'he loves her too much. That was quite obvious.'

'Good Lord,' said Lana, 'I still can't believe it.'

'Well now,' said Hilary opening her handbag. 'Brace yourselves for a *real* shock.'

Rory leant over his wife's shoulder to see the news sheet Hilary had given her. At first they neither of them recognised Maxine in the picture. They saw the head and shoulders of a glowing girl with a saucy chic hair-do dancing in the arms of a man who was smiling into her eyes. Rory was the first to find his voice.

'Christ! Is that really Maxine?'

Lana tore her gaze away from the picture. 'What does it say, Mother? My French isn't too hot.'

'Well,' said Hilary, 'the heading is "Their First Tango in Paris". Then it goes on "the tango being expertly performed last night at the Colette Foundation Ball by lovely Maxine French of Hilary French Modes and that well-known man-about-town—photographer Paul O'Rourke. Will wedding bells shortly be ringing for this glamorous duo?"'

'And will they?' asked Lana, staring down at her sister's picture.

'I don't think so,' said Hilary, 'somehow I don't think so. By the way, Maxine's not coming home for Christmas this year. She's going with Paul to stay with his mother in Nice. She wondered if you would both like to visit her for a weekend before Christmas to exchange presents. She's got a spare room in her apartment.'

'Try and stop us,' said Lana, 'this I must see for myself.' Sobering suddenly she asked, 'Did Maxine say anything about Alan Maxwell or his child?'

'No,' said Hilary, 'not a word. She seemed completely wrapped up in her life in Paris and Paul. Solange Dupont says it's been almost like a miracle.'

'Takes a man,' said Rory smugly. 'I think this calls for another drink.'

CHAPTER TWENTY FIVE

And now it was spring again. Alan paused to look at the daffodils standing bravely in the rain. Gail had planted the daffodils when they first moved into the house although, by the time they bloomed, she had been too sick to get much joy from them. Gail, she seemed such a long way out of his life now. He had, during the last few months, done what he had told Bill Brandon he wanted to do, helled around, spent weekends with willing partners in plush hotels, slept late, a free man. His house was in order now, thanks to his aunt Molly. She had refused to return herself, but had found him a capable widow of sixty to act as housekeeper; and she, with the help of a 'daily', ran the household and cared for Patsy. Patsy had seemed none the worse for her exposure the night Cleo had left her alone in the house and appeared content enough with Mrs Fogarty whom she called 'Foggy'. Patsy was an aloof child, but although she didn't smile a lot, she didn't seem unhappy.

Alan on this wet spring morning was a restless, unhappy man. The freedom had soon gone sour. Apart from his job, he had no purpose in life. It was obvious, he thought, that Patsy would grow up self-sufficient and, after the way she'd been pushed around, who could blame her?

An unfamiliar sound assailed his ears as he entered the house. Patsy was giggling, in fact she was laughing.

'See,' said a voice he hadn't heard for too long, 'see, she even puts her tongue out, and look at her frilly knickers, aren't they just trendy? Her name is Monique and she was born in France where I live now. I know, Patsy, we'll introduce her to Teddy and Betsy-Ann, shall we?'

Alan stood in the doorway looking down at Maxine sitting on the floor holding up a ridiculous looking doll. Patsy was on the floor, too, with another doll and a teddy-bear. Maxine, in tight jeans and a sloppy sweater looked, he thought, like Patsy's elder sister. The smile died on her lips as she looked up at him. Now was testing time and Maxine was ready.

'Hello Alan,' she said quietly.

'Maxine!' He swooped down, caught her under the arms and hauled her to her feet. 'Maxine, how very, very good to see you.'

'Is it?' she said coolly, releasing herself, 'how nice of you to say so.'

His gaze travelled over her from head to foot. Maxine had always worn the right clothes, but this girl in her casual gear staring at him so dispassionately was not the Maxine he knew. Her hair was saucily cut making her look ridiculously young, her lovely eyes held a permanent hint of amusement, the whole presence of her was different. He decided he didn't like it, yet, oddly, it excited him. Maxine, the quiet, elegant girl had become a glossy Parisian doll like the one she now passed to Patsy. That's the word, he thought unhappily, glossy, and so bloody sure of herself like she'd never been before.

'You've changed, Maxine.'

Her smile widened slightly. 'About time, wouldn't you say? I was rather like the old song, wasn't I? Stay at home, play at home, sleepy town gal.'

'I liked the sleepy town gal,' he said gravely. 'Maxine, are you home for good now?'

'Oh no,' she said, 'just a flying visit, no pun intended. I'm going back tomorrow.'

His face fell.

'I got in late last night,' she continued, 'I saw this doll at the airport and I knew I just had to get it for Patsy.'

She spoke easily and carelessly, this new Maxine. There was no hint of reproach in her manner towards him. He thought, with an odd feeling of resentment, it's almost as if she didn't care about Cleo.

'Why can't you stay, Maxine?'

She met his gaze levelly. 'There's nothing for me here. My life is in Paris now.'

'Maxine . . .' She turned away as he put out a hand towards her.

'That's it, Patsy,' she said, 'make teddy give her a big kiss.'

'I suppose you've got lots of friends in Paris?'

'Of course,' she replied simply, 'I'd be lonely

otherwise, wouldn't I?'

Jealousy was a pain inside him as he blurted out savagely, 'And I bet you're not lonely.'

With a tiny, secret smile she said softly, 'No, I'm never lonely.'

'Lots of friends? *Just* friends?'

'And Jupiter and Jezebel,' she said, 'a cat and a car.'

'Why won't you be serious, Maxine?'

She looked at him with innocent eyes. 'Why should I? Why should I answer all these questions?'

He gave a great sigh and his shoulders slumped. 'No,' he said, 'why the hell should you? I wrote to you, you know, twice, care of your mother's salon, but you didn't reply.'

'There seemed no point,' she said.

'Oh Maxine!' he cried, 'I've missed you, like hell I've missed you, every day and in every way since the day you left and that's God's truth.'

His impassioned declaration appeared to have fallen on deaf ears because Maxine reached for the teddy-bear and said, 'Look, his ribbon needs tightening, Patsy.' Then she looked back at Alan. 'I'll leave you my card,' she said coolly, 'look me up some time when you visit Paris.'

Patsy looked up from her dolls, her mouth turning down as she realised Maxine wasn't staying.

'Masseen, don't go 'way again, Masseen.'

Maxine smiled fondly down at her. 'I have to

go, darling, back to my work, but I have an idea, how about you coming to stay with me at my home in Paris for a little holiday?' She glanced at Alan. 'That is, if Daddy can spare you.'

'I'll deliver her myself,' he offered eagerly. That's it, he thought suddenly, if Patsy's the only way to get her, I'll get her through Patsy, but get her I bloody well will and she won't get away next time. Then reason said, she didn't get away last time, you *sent* her and now it might be too late. It mustn't be too late. I know now that I've loved her ever since she first started caring for Gail, my lovely Maxine.

'That's it then, darling,' Maxine said to the child, 'I'll take some time off and we'll go to all sorts of lovely places in Paris where I live, and there's a beautiful pussy-cat called Jupiter who comes into my home. You'll love him and we'll have such a lot of fun, sweetheart.'

'Tomorrow?'

Maxine laughed. 'Not exactly tomorrow, pet, but very, very soon, I promise. Smile, Patsy, we don't have long faces where *I* live.'

'Can Teddy and Betsy-Ann and . . .' the child stopped, having already forgotten the name of her new doll.

'Monique,' supplied Maxine, 'yes, they can all come, Teddy, Betsy-Ann and Monique. You can all come in Daddy's aeroplane.' Her gaze swivelled to Alan. 'Captain's baggage, right, Alan?'

He fought down the desire to seize her and

kiss that bloody infuriating smile off her mouth.

'What do *you* know about Captain's baggage?' he demanded curtly.

'I've learnt a lot in Paris.'

'I'll bet you have,' he retorted bitterly. 'Tell me it's none of my damn business, Maxine, if you like, but is there someone special for you in Paris?'

'Yes,' she said simply, 'someone *very* special.'

Despair dragged him down. 'You're going to marry him?'

She made him wait for her answer, then she shook her head. 'No, I'm not going to marry him.'

'Shack up, I suppose? That's the done thing these days and I should know, shouldn't I?'

He ran his hands distractedly through his hair and she wanted so much to go and smooth it down for him.

'I suppose you're shacked up already?'

'No,' she said, 'I live alone. We are not, and never will be, lovers.'

Relief flooded over him and he had a sudden savage desire to hurt her.

'Well, whoever he is, he's changed you, Maxine. You've changed almost beyond recognition, not only in appearance, but in yourself, it's . . . it's almost as if you don't care Maxine, I don't like it.'

'Don't you?' she said, amusement in her eyes, 'then you must tell him so when you meet him.'

The laughter faded from her eyes. 'You see, Alan,' she said, 'wherever I go, whatever I do, he will always be a very big part of my life.'

She moved to the window and looked out. 'See,' she said, 'it's spring again. It's stopped raining.'

We hope you have enjoyed this Large Print book. Other Chivers Press or G.K. Hall & Co. Large Print books are available at your library or directly from the publishers.

For more information about current and forthcoming titles, please call or write, without obligation, to:

Chivers Press Limited
Windsor Bridge Road
Bath BA2 3AX
England
Tel. (01225) 335336

OR

G.K. Hall & Co.
P.O. Box 159
Thorndike, Maine 04986
USA
Tel. (800) 223-2336

All our Large Print titles are designed for easy reading, and all our books are made to last.